Counting Stars

BY

L. D. K. JOHNSON

Sometimes life doesn't work out the way you imagine,

but it works out the way it is supposed to...

This is a work of fiction. Names, characters, businesses, places, events, locales, and incidents are either the products of the author's imagination or used in a fictitious manner. Any resemblance to actual persons, living or dead, hapless stargazer, or actual events or places is purely coincidental.

ISBN: 978-1-959715-18-4

Library of Congress Control Number: **2023940777**

Published by **Belen Books, LLC**

7901 4th St. N, Ste 300, St. Petersburg, FL. 33702 USA

Belenbookspublishing.com

Edited by Beverly R. Waalewyn and Paul Hight
Cover by Belen Media Group
Title facing page quote by L.D.K Johnson

Printed in the United States of America

Dedication

To all the strong-willed, courageous women

who live and love with all their hearts.

Counting Stars

Prologue

"What are you doing up there?"

Ian stared at the little girl perched on top of her roof, staring at the night sky, long black hair flowing around her slender face. Her pink princess pajamas were the only protection against the cool autumn breeze.

"Get down," he urged, feeling his heartbeat accelerate. "You're gonna fall."

Ignoring the little boy's request, Asa continued her evening ritual.

The sky tonight was breathtaking. The heavenly canvas was filled with thousands of twinkling lights. All were illuminating the dark expanse until it shone.

According to her parents, the view alone was worth moving from Detroit to Denver. Of course, she still missed Tanya, Maribel, and Paula with all of her heart, but there was no comparing the brilliance of a clear night sky from a mountain top rather than the bowels of a congested city.

"Are you crazy?" the boy bellowed from below, the anxiety in his voice clear. "If you don't come down…"

He paused, debating his next words.

"I'm coming up!"

Silence battered his ears.

Great!

Now he'd have to go up.

Looking around, he found a long, metallic ladder leaning against the side wall of the well-kept two-story, yellow-and-white contemporary home. The house, although large and immaculately maintained, had been empty for almost a year. The last owners were an old married couple who retired to Florida to be near their children and to get away from the harsh Colorado winters.

Ian had seen the moving trucks earlier in the week but hadn't caught a glimpse of the people who had purchased the house. He was curious. He'd hoped it was a couple with children his age that he could play with. It was a lonely existence he led as an only child of two working professionals living in an area where the closest neighbor with kids was over a mile away.

He wanted a friend.

No, he needed a friend. At this point in time, he was even willing to settle for a strange girl who didn't speak and who liked to lay on her roof. He'd take what he could and make the best of it. After all, that's what he always did.

Slowly and with great care, Ian climbed the ladder and stood precariously at the edge of the roof. Nervously, he concentrated… *Don't look down…* What was he thinking? He knew he was deathly afraid of heights, so what in the world was he doing standing on this odd girl's roof?

Taking a shaky breath, he said, "Hi. I'm Ian… Ian Granger. I live across the street."

Still no response. Maybe she was mute. Or she couldn't speak English.

"Can you speak?" the thought spilled out of his mouth. "Do you understand English?"

He was running out of questions.

Finally, the girl turned. She was not very pretty. Her face was sullen and pale, with dark circles shadowing her dark brown, almost onyx eyes. Her mouth was pursed, and the look of annoyance she gave him was almost enough to send him fleeing from his wobbly position beside her.

"I understand you," she whispered, her voice emotionless.

"What are you doing up here?" Ian blurted.

He wanted to sit down but was terrified to move lest he fall.

After a long pause, she finally answered.

"Counting stars."

"Oh," he replied, finding the idea of counting so many stars a bit crazy. Then again, she seemed a bit crazy. So, he guessed it was perfectly normal… for her.

"Do you know this is really dangerous?" he asked with a sigh.

The girl watched him curiously but still gave no signal he should continue with his chastisement.

"If you come down, we can play Nintendo or something."

Turning away, she resumed her previous endeavor of staring at the night sky.

~ iv ~

"If you ever want to talk, you know where I live."

Nothing.

Girls!

Always so difficult.

Turning slowly, he backtracked down the ladder, giving a relieved sigh when his Converse touched the grass-covered ground. He'd finally gotten a neighbor his age or close to it, and she was nuts. The universe had a strange sense of humor.

"Asa, who was that boy?" her mother questioned from below, dark eyes fixed on her five-year-old, a lovely smile graced her full pink lips.

Asa smiled.

"That was Ian. My new friend."

~ V ~

Chapter One

Five years later…

"Asa!" The familiar voice called to her from across the schoolyard. "Wait up!"

Ian's briskly moving form approached. Dark hair longer than it should be hitting the collar of his blue polo, blue eyes shining, and a look of amusement on his dirt-streaked face.

"What have you been doing?"

She frowned at the sight of his bruised knees and mud-covered sneakers.

"Rolling around in the mud, I'm guessing," she teased, continuing her walk toward the pick-up / drop-off area where her mom would be collecting them.

"How'd you do on the math test?" he ignored her comment, arranging his bulging backpack more securely over one shoulder.

"I think I did okay," she replied, biting her bottom lip nervously.

"You always say that," he smirked, nudging her gently with his elbow. "And you always end up acing it."

"What can I say?" she added with a cocky chuckle. "I'm gifted."

"Yeah, right," he snickered loudly, making her roll her eyes.

"Hey, Ian!" Brian Wilson, Ian's baseball teammate, called to him. The boy was accompanied by two other dirty ten-year-olds who also looked like they'd gone rolling in the mud as well. "Wanna practice hitting some fastballs?"

"I can't," he informed, shaking his head. "I've got homework."

"Hi, Asa," Brian acknowledged her with a timid expression.

Ian wasn't surprised when Asa's eyes narrowed into thin daggers of irritation, causing the other boy to physically recoil. She and Brian Wilson had a mutual hate/hate relationship which had started the first day she attended Eleanor Roosevelt Elementary School five years ago. She still remembered Brian pushing her on the playground during recess and then calling her an extremely nasty word before grabbing her snack of peanut butter crackers out of her hand as she lay sprawled in the mulch.

Without hesitation, she turned away, leaving the boys talking, wanting to leave Brian and his group of minions as quickly as possible.

"I'll meet you at the pick-up line," she announced solemnly.

"Okay," Ian's voice dropped an octave, and his eyes narrowed curiously at her quickly retreating form.

A sigh of relief escaped as she made her way away from the small group. Being within hitting distance of the boy who had single-handedly ruined her first day at a new school was enough to make her violent. It was no secret she'd often pictured hitting the hyped-up fifth grader with her unnaturally heavy backpack.

Unfortunately, Brian was Ian's friend, and she didn't want to cause a rift between the two. So instead of giving in to her baser instincts, she avoided him as much as she could. Unsubtly, she made it a point to leave the room whenever he entered, unless they were in class, and often held her tongue... which was an impressive feat for her. Of course, she still felt obligated to ignore him or glare evilly at him.

A barrage of memories from that day filled her mind causing her to grimace.

Thank goodness for Ian. The incident on the playground during their kindergarten year was the first and last time Brian ever touched her or called her a bad word. Ian had seen the entire incident from his position on the monkey bars, ran over, and punched the other boy so hard he knocked his front tooth loose. After that, Brian kept his distance. And Ian, the eternal optimist, reluctantly accepted the fact that Asa despised his teammate and made no attempt at hiding her feelings.

A few minutes later, Ian caught up to her, hair messy and falling into his eyes. *Boys!* She'd never figure them out.

"Why are you walking so fast?"

Curiosity got the best of her.

"What was that all about?" she interrogated, ignoring his question.

"They wanted to invite me to play baseball this Saturday afternoon," he replied, shrugging his shoulders halfheartedly. "You wanna come with me?"

Adamantly, she shook her head in response.

"Why not?"

No answer.

"It'll be fun," Ian insisted. "You can sit in the stands and cheer me on."

"That doesn't sound like much fun to me," she glared, dark eyes fixed on him, and he wanted to curl into a ball like a pill bug. For some reason, she'd always intimidated him even though she was short for her age and underweight. Also, Asa seldom spoke, at least to other people. Sometimes not even to him.

"Do you have another doctor's appointment?" he added.

His lungs tightened at the idea of Asa having to go back to the hospital to run more tests.

Instinctively, her hands clutched the straps of her backpack, knuckles turning white from the force of her grip.

"Yeah," she whispered, staring at nothing.

"Would you like me to come with you?" he volunteered as concern spread across his facial features.

He'd always asked, and she'd always said no.

"It's okay," she grinned, trying to be brave, but her eyes gave her away. "Have fun with the guys. There's no point of us both having a terrible weekend."

Ian's chest tightened.

"Have they found out if it's back?"

Asa had been diagnosed with acute lymphoblastic leukemia six years ago before they had met. She'd been in and out of hospitals for as long as he knew her. Every time she went for her biannual check-up, he'd worry she'd tell him it had returned. Fortunately, she had been in remission since then, but you just never knew.

His best friend was the bravest person he'd ever known. Needles didn't bother her. Hospitals didn't give her hives. Not even chemotherapy had scared her. Or at least she never acted like it did. In his opinion, she was even more courageous than his dad, and that was saying something. His father was a fireman and ran into burning buildings for a living. He'd even gotten a special award for saving a family when their cabin caught fire while they were camping at Rocky Mountain National Park.

That year was crazy. Reporters wanted to do articles about his father and their family. News stations asked for television interviews. His dad even got to speak at the annual fireman's banquet. Ian had been extremely proud.

"I have a few more tests to take," her voice softened. Looking up at him, she gave a rare smile; the simple act transformed her face into a work of art. "Don't worry so much. You're worse than my parents."

Mr. and Mrs. Addams treated their only daughter, only child, with kid gloves, never allowing her to do anything that would put her at risk. Unfortunately, most things children liked to do *were* dangerous, which made them fun.

"You're my best friend," he reminded, reaching for her backpack, knowing it was too heavy for her to carry comfortably. "I'm supposed to worry about you."

"Huh," she scoffed, earning her one of his patented arched eyebrows, reminding her of Mr. Spock from Star Trek. "The only reason you're my best friend is because you're in love with my mom's cooking."

"That's not true," he denied.

Although truthfully, Mrs. Addams was the best cook he'd ever met. Her chocolate chip cookies were legendary throughout the county and were usually the first things to sell out at school bake sales. Fortunately for him, he lived across the street and was best friends with Asa, so he got cookies straight from the oven whenever he wanted.

Mrs. Addams also made amazing Japanese food, which being Japanese-American, explained why, but she also excelled at every other kind of cuisine as well. No doubt it was because she had graduated from the legendary *Le Cordon Bleu* in Paris and worked as a restaurant chef before she met and married Asa's dad.

Mr. Addams, a meteorologist who worked for the Space Weather Prediction Center in Boulder, a part of the National Weather Service, was the reason Asa loved to lie on her roof counting stars. Her dad, an amateur astronomer, started doing the strange ritual after she had been diagnosed with cancer as a child. It was a custom Asa had shared with him.

Unfortunately, Ian was still afraid of heights, but counting stars on Asa's roof was something he looked forward to. In his mind, if Asa could do it, so could he. She inspired him. Although, he would never tell her that.

"That's not the only reason why we're friends," he admitted shyly.

"Sure," she mocked. "If there was another person our age that lived close by, you'd ditch me in a heartbeat."

It was how she felt. Asa always spoke her mind, even if it hurt other people's feelings. She didn't mean to be harsh. It was just her way.

"Whatever you say," he mumbled, staring at the concrete sidewalk below his feet. "Do you want me to come over Saturday night?"

The girl remained silent.

"We could go up on the roof..." he shuffled his feet nervously.

"I'll call you if I'm up to it," Asa quickly replied, also looking down. "You know how I get after all of those tests."

He did know. She was always tired and cranky. Who wouldn't be after being poked and prodded all day by various hospital staff?

"My mom's here." She nodded in the direction of the black Toyota Sienna pulling into the school parking lot, ending their conversation.

Dinner at the Addams' house was always delicious. Mrs. Addams made homemade macaroni and cheese, mini meatloaves with a sweet and spicy glaze, and sautéed baby carrots. He had three helpings and still wasn't full.

"Don't fill up," Mrs. Addams warned. "There's fresh baked apple pie with vanilla ice cream for dessert."

Immediately, Ian leaned over.

"If your parents ever get divorced, I'm gonna marry your mom," he whispered to Asa.

"Eww," she grimaced at the very disturbing thought.

"Did you finish all of your homework?" Mr. Addams asked, looking at both of them.

"I have a timeline to complete, and then I'm finished," Ian informed, feeling pleased with himself.

Asa, on the other hand, shifted uncomfortably in her seat.

"I have to study for a vocabulary test, and I still have my timeline to do."

"Do you need some help studying?" her dad inquired.

She shook her head.

"If you change your mind, I'll be in my office reading some astronomy articles. There's meant to be a meteor shower this Saturday," Mr. Addams grinned like a schoolboy finding a box of chocolate bars.

"Have you ever seen a meteor shower, Ian?" Mrs. Addams queried as she gathered the empty dishes. Asa stood to help her, but her mother waved her away. His friend plopped back down on the dining chair with a huff.

"No, ma'am," he admitted. "But I'd like to."

"Come over around nine Saturday night." Mr. Addams studied his daughter's odd reaction to his invitation with a strange look on his face. "If your parents agree you can watch it with us. Wouldn't that be nice, Asa?"

The shrugging of her shoulders was the only answer she gave.

"I'd like that," Ian beamed.

"I'll make a batch of chocolate chip cookies for the event." Mrs. Addams announced, then disappeared into the kitchen.

"May we please be excused?" Asa began fidgeting in her seat again. "We have to finish our homework."

"Sure, honey," her father smiled sweetly, returning his attention to the last bite of meatloaf on his plate.

Obediently, Ian followed Asa to the living room, where their books were laid out.

"I can't wait to see the meteor shower." He observed her, trying to gauge her mood. "Your mom making cookies is a bonus."

Asa resumed her homework, completely ignoring him.

"What's the matter?"

"Nothing," she grumbled, avoiding eye contact.

Sitting next to her, he disregarded her growl of annoyance.

"C'mon, tell me what's wrong," he urged, having no idea what was bothering her.

"I'm afraid." She looked past his shoulder at something behind him on the wall.

"Of what?" he asked, taking one of her much smaller hands in his.

A few years ago, he would never have touched her. Everyone knew back then that girls had cooties.

A mournful sigh escaped her lips.

"I'll find out the results of the tests on Saturday," she prompted.

"Right," his voice lowered like they were in church. "I forgot."

He tried to find something to say to lighten the mood, but for the life of him, he couldn't think of anything. Truthfully, he was nervous to learn about the results as well.

Lately, Asa had gotten tired easily. She didn't eat as much as she should. Her skin was pale and sickly. She was not the picture of health. But then again, she'd always been this way… even after she went into remission.

"Suppose they say it's back." The grip on her standard number two pencil tightened. "Suppose I have to do chemo again. Suppose I—"

"Stop supposing," he interrupted, gently squeezing her hand. "If it's back, I'll be right here with you… taking care of you. I'll bring you your homework and give you the 411 on all the drama at school."

Suddenly, she smiled. A lovely smile that made his chest tighten.

Clearing his throat, he continued: "Now, let's get back to this boring timeline."

Chapter Two

"You're out!" Brian yelled from his position behind home plate. "What's with you today, Ian? You're meant to be hitting the ball, not staring off into space."

"Sorry!" he yelled back, his mind with Asa at the hospital.

Absent-mindedly, Ian glanced at his watch.

"I've gotta go."

"Going to see your girlfriend?" Brian's body stiffened when his friend shot him a warning glare. "Are you playing with us next weekend?"

"I'll see," Ian responded. "Depends on how Asa's tests are."

Brian shook his head.

"Is she okay?" the other boy questioned with genuine concern.

"I don't know," Ian grimaced at the possibilities. "She finds out today."

"Tell her," the young man began but suddenly stopped. "On the other hand, don't tell her I said anything."

Ian's brow hitched.

"You know she doesn't like me."

"I wonder why," Ian chuckled.

Avoiding eye contact, Brian kicked at the ground with the toe of his cleats.

"I was five—"

"I know," he interrupted, handing Brian the bat. "But Asa doesn't forget or forgive easily."

"Anyway, I hope she's all right," his friend mumbled, the look on his face sincere.

"Me too," Ian agreed.

An annoyed Asa leered at him as he cleared the last rung of the ladder.

"You're late," she informed with a huff.

"I know. I had to clean my room before I could come over," he admitted breathlessly, sitting beside him; a plush blanket made the spot more comfortable. "I didn't miss it, did I?"

"No," she replied with an almost inaudible grunt.

"How did it go at the hospital?" he grilled, unable to beat around the bush.

"Not good," she grumbled, continuing to stare at the sky.

"When do you start chemo?" he probed, grabbing her hand.

"Next week," she announced, wiping away the first tear.

Before he could comfort her, the tears were rolling down her cheeks, so he reached over without permission and wiped them away.

"I won't be at school for a while," Asa updated him on what was about to transpire. "The medicine makes me sick, so my mom is gonna home-school me for the rest of the year."

"I'll miss you… at school, that is," the boy frowned. "But I'm going to visit you every day—"

"No." She stared at him with weepy eyes. "Don't visit me."

"Why not?" One dark brow hitched.

Asa tried pulling her hand away, but he held it tighter.

"I don't want visitors because I don't want you to see me like that," Asa mumbled.

"Like what?"

"Pale and sickly and—"

His brow hitched again, and this time, he smirked.

"I look even worse," she replied, rolling her eyes.

He opened his mouth to say something and was cut off.

"Don't say anything smart, or I'll push you off of this roof."

Her words weren't accompanied by a smile, so he knew not to attempt a joke.

With that stated, Ian released her hand so he could lay on the blanket and then wait as she did the same.

"I'm gonna miss this," the boy confessed.

"Me too," she admitted solemnly as the first meteor streaked the heavens. "Mom! Dad!" she shouted. "It's starting!"

Patiently, they waited while Asa's parents joined them. All four stared up at the clear night sky in comfortable silence, watching the celestial light show in wonder.

"I know how I can still be with you," the determined boy suddenly announced.

Intrigued by his declaration, Asa turned to look at him.

"How?"

"We'll call each other when we want to watch the stars, then we'll both go up on our roofs," he stated, pointing toward his roof. "I can see you from my house."

Smiling brightly, Asa agreed.

"We can get walkie-talkies, too," he continued. "That way, we can talk to each other."

The longing in her eyes was not hidden from him, and he turned away, afraid she'd see his eyes welling. He wasn't going to cry in front of her. He had promised himself years ago that she'd never see him cry. She had enough to deal with.

"Cookies?" Mrs. Addams offered them a Tupperware container of her famous baked dessert.

Eagerly, he grabbed one and then took a large bite.

"Delicious," he moaned. It was still warm.

"Mmm," Asa moaned too, and reached for another.

Amused by the children's enthusiasm, Mr. and Mrs. Addams laughed as they helped themselves to cookies as well.

"Mmm," they both hummed in unison.

Suddenly, Asa pointed to the streaks of light across the night sky.

"Look, there's another!"

Sure enough, the sky resembled a painter's canvas streaked with white paint against the black background. Tonight, was one he'd never forget, sitting on Asa's roof, eating cookies, and watching his first meteor shower. He'd remember this moment for the rest of his life.

Chapter Three

"Asa… come in, Asa," Ian spoke into the walkie-talkie awaiting his friend's voice.

"Hold your horses," Asa's voice finally came through the small hand-held device. "You're so impatient. Jeez!"

Her exasperated words made him smile.

It had been almost a month since he'd seen her last. They spoke each night via the walkie-talkies, but it wasn't the same. Several times he had asked if he could visit, but each time she refused. Even after he had informed her that he didn't care if she looked like a hideous beast or not, that comment earned him a maniacal laugh and a seething speech.

"What's taking so long?" he probed, watching her climb through the attic window out onto the slightly sloping roof.

"The treatments make me weak," her breathy gasps filled his ears and saddened his heart.

"I'm sorry," he winced, feeling like an idiot for not realizing the strains her body was going through.

"Why?" she inquired sweetly, so in contrast to her last statement.

Girls.

Their moods changed like the weather.

"It's not your fault. I feel bad."

"I know," he paused, trying to think of a way to lighten the mood. "I've been dying to tell you about P.E. today."

"What happened in P.E.?"

Thankfully, her breathing sounded normal once again. She was sitting on her favorite cushion, wrapped in a blanket, speaking into the receiver and watching him. It wasn't the same as when they were together, but it was better than nothing.

"Misty Ryan got hit in the face with a basketball," he snorted loudly.

"Good!" Asa snorted back; her mood lifted.

"Everyone cracked up!"

"Was she all right?" her tone sounded more sympathetic.

"Yeah, it didn't break anything," he chuckled. "But she did walk around for the rest of the day with a big red mark on her forehead."

They both laughed.

"It was hilarious!" Ian smirked as he tried not to snort again.

"I wish I was there to see it," the girl giggled.

"Me too."

Then he heard her sniffle but didn't mention it. She would only deny it and get upset.

"Asa?"

"Yeah?" his friend muttered softly.

"Why do you and Misty hate each other?"

Anxiously, Ian waited through the long, tense silence as she seemed to mull over his question.

"It's a long story," she finally huffed.

"We have time," he encouraged. "Tell me."

"Did we come up here to talk or count stars?" she countered in her blunt way.

"Both," he informed as he watched her from afar.

"Look!" she pointed toward the sky, completely changing the subject. "It's a shooting star!"

"Make a wish," he requested in a hushed tone.

"We'll both wish," she informed. "Are you ready?"

"Uh-huh."

"Close your eyes," she ordered, doing the same. "Ok, make your wish."

After a few seconds, she opened her eyes.

"What did you wish for?"

"I can't tell," he chuckled.

"Why not?"

He could imagine her rolling her eyes.

"Because if I tell you, it won't come true."

"Oh, yeah," Asa smirked cheerfully. "Ian?"

"Huh?"

"Thank you," the girl whispered into the device.

"*Shhh*, I'm concentrating," he teased.

They both laughed, then went back to counting stars.

Chapter Four

Five years later...

"Asa, hurry up!" Ian shouted. "You're making us late!"

He still couldn't figure out why girls took so long to get ready.

"I'm gonna leave without you."

"Fine!" she yelled back. "Go ahead! I'll catch up!"

"You know I'm not gonna leave you," he stressed, folding his arms across his chest.

"I know," she replied with a snicker.

"Brian's party started at six," he reminded, his left foot tapping his annoyance. "It's almost six thirty."

There was silence.

"Asa Francesca Addams, get your butt down here this minute."

Still, there was no answer.

Confusion settled upon him.

It always worked when her parents said it.

"Stop yelling," Asa's calm voice came from the direction of the stairs. "I'm ready."

Ian turned to face her.

"It's about time—" his rebuke stopped in midsentence as he stared at his best friend waiting on the fourth step. "Holy cow," he mumbled below his breath.

"Well?" She turned around to show off her new dress. "How do I look?"

For the life of him, he couldn't come up with one appropriate word to describe how she looked except, *Damn.*

Her eyes narrowed.

"If it looks that bad, I can change; just give me a few more minutes—"

"No," he snapped, mouth going dry. "It's fine."

Truthfully, it was better than fine. It was gorgeous. Asa was gorgeous.

"Are you sure it's appropriate? I've never worn a formal gown before. I wish I was back in my jeans and t-shirt."

Mesmerized, Ian continued to stare, unable to look away.

"Stop staring at me like that," she ordered, folding her arms over the bodice of her dress, the motion calling attention to her ample cleavage.

"C'mon." He motioned toward the door, trying to get his treacherous member under control. "My parents are waiting in the car."

"Wait." A deep voice halted them as Mr. and Mrs. Addams appeared, Mr. Addams holding a camera in his hand. "We need to take some pictures."

"You two are embarrassing me," Asa rolled her eyes. "We don't need to take pictures."

"Yes, we do," her mom gently informed.

"It's not like we're going to prom," she reminded with an exasperated huff.

"This is the first time both of you have gotten dressed up," her mother professed on a sigh. "Usually, you live in jeans and t-shirts."

Then Mrs. Addams turned to Ian and frowned.

"And Ian doesn't care what he wears."

"I care," he blushed at the woman's comment.

"We could have taken a hundred pictures by now if you'd stop arguing with your mother," Mr. Addams' tone dripped with irritation.

"Okay, If you insist," Asa grumbled as she came downstairs to stand beside her friend.

"Get closer, you two," Mr. Addams requested.

They followed his instructions without complaint, stopping when their shoulders touched.

Suddenly, the delicate scent of roses filled his nostrils.

"Are you wearing perfume?" he questioned, drawn to the fragrance of the heady concoction. In actuality, he was drawn to Asa.

To his surprise, his mercurial friend looked stunning wearing a strapless, royal blue party dress with delicate strands of silver thread embroidered into the semi-glossy material. Two-inch silver heels and understated silver earrings and a necklace completed her outfit. Her make-up was perfectly done but not too heavy, allowing her beauty to shine through. Ebony locks meticulously straightened cascaded to the middle of her back, beckoning him to touch—of course—he didn't.

"Closer," Mrs. Addams encouraged; unknown to the woman, his member had awakened and refused to go back to its former flaccid state. Subtly, he arranged his blazer to cover the errant appendage.

"Any closer, and we'll be conjoined twins," Asa giggled, the sound lancing his cock like a sword.

"We're really late," he reminded, trying to avoid any further scrutiny.

"Sorry," her mother apologized. "Just one more."

Without delay, Mr. Addams snapped several pictures.

"Last one," Asa's father informed. "Ian, put your arm around Asa's waist. Asa, sweetheart, put your hand on his chest."

Asa's eyes widened to the size of her mom's chocolate chip cookies.

"No," she huffed. "No more pictures."

To tell the truth, Ian didn't know whether to be offended or relieved.

"Asa," Mrs. Addams scolded. "Do as your father says."

Reluctantly, she did as she was told, hands trembling at the idea of being so close to her best friend, a best friend who knew all of her secrets but didn't know how much she liked him. No. Not like. That wasn't a strong enough word for what she felt for Ian Granger. It was love. Of that, she was certain.

"Good grief, Asa," Ian growled. "Do you have to argue over everything?"

Before she could answer, he impatiently grabbed her and hauled her against his chest, which for some unknown reason, was slightly heaving. Quickly, he wound one muscular arm around her waist, securing her in place. Hesitantly, she leaned closer, resting her open palm on his lapel.

Asa had to admit; he looked dashing tonight in his brand-new gray suit, royal blue dress shirt that brought out his intense blue eyes, gray tie, and black dress shoes. When she first saw him, she had to hold on to the banister to keep upright. The sight of him stole her breath and her heart.

"Perfect." Her dad smiled as he snapped the final picture. "Let your parents know I'll email them the photos of the two of you."

"I will." Ian offered her his arm, but she obstinately refused, stepping around him instead. He didn't care. From his position behind her, he had the best view of her slightly swaying ass.

Glorious.

"Don't forget, home by midnight," Mrs. Addams reminded. They both nodded their understanding. "Have fun. Remember to stay on the sidewalk… no wandering off… stay together."

"Keiko," Mr. Addams soothed, giving her a gentle hug. "They'll be fine. They're almost sixteen. She'll be home before you know it."

Asa gave her parents quick hugs before they left.

"See you later," she smiled.

"Have fun," her parents replied at the same time.

"Ian," Mr. Addams halted their retreat. "Take care of my daughter."

Ian beamed.

"Always."

Everything was better than she could have ever imagined. The recreational center, which normally smelled of *Icy-Hot* and mint, was beautifully decorated with festive balloons, neon streamers, and even a disco ball hung above the parquet floors, bathing dancers below with multicolored dots of light.

"Wow!" Asa's grip tightened on her evening clutch. "This place looks incredible."

Ian had to agree.

"There's Brian," he informed, waving at the teen who was chatting with a group of similarly dressed partygoers. "Let's say hello."

"I don't know," Asa whispered. "I feel kinda strange being here. Brian and I aren't exactly friends."

Reassuringly, Ian took her hand and guided her across the room.

"You and Brian are on good terms now, right?"

"Right," she repeated, trying to calm the nervous butterflies in her stomach.

"He wouldn't have invited you to his sixteenth birthday party if he didn't think of you as a friend, right?"

"Right," she agreed again, tightening her grip on his hand.

Brian smiled when he saw them approaching.

"Hey, guys," he greeted, shaking Ian's hand before he turned to her and stopped.

The other young man's mouth gaped as his eyes raked her from head to toe, then back again.

"Asa," he gulped, clearing his throat. "You look absolutely gorgeous."

"Thanks." A blush stole across her face. "You look terrific too."

"You like it?" Brian confidently adjusted his jacket, making her giggle. "Save a dance for me tonight."

"Maybe," Asa's blush deepened.

"Maybe?" Brian unapologetically flirted. "Don't break my heart, Asa."

Ian's eyes narrowed suspiciously at them.

"Do you want something to eat?" Ian asked, interrupting their playful banter.

Still embarrassed, she nodded.

"I'll get you some—"

"I'll take her to the buffet," Brian offered a little too enthusiastically for his liking, eyes still glued to Asa's flushed face. "After you."

The teen motioned her ahead, and instantly, his eyes lowered to Asa's tempting ass. It was all Ian could do not to attack a long-time friend in the middle of the festivities.

"She looks tasty," Billy Morgan sneered.

"Yeah," Edward Finney agreed; both stared at Asa's retreating form. "Who knew she would turn into such a hottie."

"Shut up," Ian ordered, elbowing the boy in the ribcage. "Stop talking about her like that."

"Like what?" Billy asked, a look of agitation on his dark features. "Asa is beautiful, smart, and available. Why shouldn't we notice?"

"Yeah, Ian," Edward spoke next. "Why shouldn't we want to ask her out?"

Unable to stop himself, Ian grabbed the boy by the lapel.

"Sorry," Edward apologized. "Do you want her? If she's yours, we'll back off."

A loud sigh escaped his lips.

"She's not mine." He released the boy and fixed his jacket. "Asa's always been delicate. You know, from cancer—"

"We know, but she's better now, and we care about her as much as you do," Edward cautiously explained.

Ian growled low.

"Okay… maybe not as much as you do," the young man continued. "But still, we're her friends too."

"What's going on, fellas?" Brian grilled as he joined the group of his close friends, hazel eyes narrowing.

"Nothing," all three answered together.

"Here," Asa's voice startled them all as she handed him a plate with an assortment of appetizers. "I thought you might be hungry."

The other guys stared at them with big smirks on their faces.

"Thanks." Looking around at the venue, he saw an empty table near the back. "Let's sit over there."

"Okay," she agreed, following him. When they were alone seated at the table, she gave him a curious stare. "What was that all about?"

Taking a rather large bite out of a deviled egg, he avoided her question along with her disciplining glare.

"They were bothering me about you," he disclosed after swallowing.

Asa forked a Swedish meatball on her plate, took a tentative bite, and then popped the remaining morsel into her mouth. Eagerly, he tasted one too.

"These aren't bad, but they're not as good as your mom's."

"What did they say?" she pried after she swallowed. She didn't really care what they said about her, but she knew Ian would.

"Nothing important," he reassured, tasting a cream-filled puff pastry; his eyes danced in delight. "Do you think your mom would teach me how to cook?"

"I don't see why not." Asa made quick work of a chilled shrimp with cocktail sauce.

Ian grinned.

"I'm thinking about becoming a chef," he paused as she digested his statement. She was silent, sizing him up in her mind. "What do you think?"

"I think you should give it a shot. After all," she giggled, "if you cook as well as you eat, you'll have your own television show on Food Network in no time."

"Ha! Ha!" he mocked, throwing his napkin at her, happy when she picked it up and threw it back. "What about you, any thoughts about what you want to be?"

"I'm thinking about photography," she stated, shrugging her shoulders.

She stilled, her hands clenching and unclenching nervously. He knew the motion well.

"I think you'd be a remarkable photographer," he praised truthfully. "You have an amazing eye for detail. You're also a perfectionist, so any picture you take will be impeccable."

Blushing, she ate another shrimp.

"Thanks for the vote of confidence."

"I'm sorry to bother you, Asa." Brian suddenly appeared beside them. "Would you like to dance?"

Ian listened to the song the DJ was playing. It was a slow song from a movie he'd seen recently with Asa. The unexpected surge of jealousy he felt startled him.

Accepting with a nod, Asa stood, allowing Brian to take her hand. Ian's brow furrowed at the simple touch.

"We'll be back," Brian divulged, but all he could do was nod.

Agitated at what he couldn't say, he sat alone for a few minutes, then decided to go outside for some air when a feminine voice called to him, causing him to turn.

"Ian," Misty Ryan gave him a dazzling smile, bringing him back from his murderous thoughts. "You're not leaving already, are you?"

"No, I need to get some air," he informed, staring at Asa and Brian dancing. It didn't help his mood that Brian was whispering something in her ear that made her laugh.

"Would you dance with me?" The teen twirled a lock of golden blonde hair around one finely manicured finger.

He didn't want to, but he agreed anyway.

"Sure, why not?"

Halfheartedly, he took Misty's hand in his and then made his way to the dance floor, stopping directly beside his friends. Immediately, Asa's gaze narrowed when she realized who his dance partner was. The two young women disliked each other, and for some reason, Asa would never tell him why, no matter how much he asked.

"You look great tonight, Ian." Misty's hands wandered down his arm to his bicep.

"You look nice too," he politely complimented as he glanced over the curvaceous creature wearing a stunning sky blue, form-fitting cocktail dress that barely covered her toned thighs he complimented.

Although, truthfully, Asa looked a hundred times better in her more conservative dress. Of course, he'd never tell Misty that. He wasn't an idiot, and he valued all of his man parts.

"You've been working out," she purred, batted her long lashes, and gave his bicep muscle a firm squeeze.

"Not really," he said in a hushed tone, hoping Asa couldn't hear their conversation. Unfortunately, the scowl on his best friend's face told him she had. Before he could remove Misty's grip from his arm Asa turned away.

Great!

He knew he'd hear about it later.

The walk back to Asa's house wasn't pleasant. Not one little bit. In fact, it was so quiet and uncomfortable that he was actually relieved to hear when his stomach started digesting his food. If not for those strange sounds, he would have gone mad.

"So," he huffed, irritation eating at his gut. "You're not talking to me now?"

Asa continued walking ahead of him, one hand clutching her small purse, the other forming into a tight fist.

"Stop being childish and talk to me."

As usual, there was no answer.

"Okay, I'll do the talking," he sighed with exasperation.

Her steps quickened.

"I'm not interested in anything you have to say," Asa growled, continuing at top speed.

"It pissed me off that you danced with Brian," he lashed out, matching her pace.

Suddenly she stopped, turning quickly on her heels, and gave him an f-off glare.

"I know I shouldn't be upset, but I am," Ian confessed, cheeks heating.

"Why?" she inquired, placing a slender hand on her hip.

"You two aren't even close," he boldly accused.

"I don't have to be *close* to someone to dance to *one* slow song."

"It was more than *one*," Ian grumbled below his breath.

"It was not," Asa argued.

"It was three," he blurted rather loudly.

"You were counting?"

Suddenly, he felt like an idiot, so he said nothing.

"I don't understand you sometimes, Ian."

"Back at ya," he grumbled, shoving his hands inside of his trouser pockets, passing her statue-like pose, refusing to look at her.

"What's that supposed to mean?" she growled, trailing a few feet behind.

"Why would you dance with someone you barely acknowledge?" he prodded. "The guy gives you one compliment, and you're all over him."

"All over him?!" her voice raised several octaves. "You've got some nerve. Brian and I had at least three to four inches between us. You and that… that… *trollop*—"

"Trollop?"

"Yes, trollop!" she spat fiercely like a cornered cobra. "You were all over each other!"

"You're nuts," he snickered, making her even angrier.

"I saw when she grabbed your arm!" her voice almost booming against the silence of the night.

"It was only an arm!"

Ian certainly couldn't tell her that Misty actually grabbed his ass after Brian and she had left the dance floor to get something to drink.

"Sure, this time it was only an arm!" she indicted vehemently.

"What about your fake high-pitched laugh every time Brian said something funny?" Ian accused, knowing that would be the winning move.

Suddenly, her heels stopped clacking against the pavement, and he knew she was stationary for the moment.

"Were you eavesdropping?"

"No," his tone reflected his growing indignation as he stopped too. "I just can't believe you flirted with *Brian*."

She gasped, annoyance fueling her rage.

"What about you?"

"What about me?"

Obviously, off his rocker, he turned to face her and made the mistake of looking at her face and wished he hadn't. The homicidal stare he encountered spoke volumes.

"What's that piece of paper in your pocket?"

Damn it!

He had forgotten Misty had written down her phone number for him to call her. He had no intention of calling, but he'd taken it anyway because he didn't want to hurt her feelings.

"That's nothing," he claimed, pulling the small scrap of paper out of his jacket pocket, surprised when Asa grabbed it out of his hand. "Give that back, Asa."

"Why?" She held it behind her back. "You wanna call your *girlfriend*?"

"Just give it back."

Turning her back to him, she read the note.

"Call me; I'd love to get to know you better… XOXO," she said in a mocking voice, trying to sound seductive and failing miserably. "What a bubblehead."

"Jealous?"

"Of who? Her?" she scoffed. "In your dreams."

"No, in reality," he taunted, trying to get the number back, but she was much too quick for him. "Don't deny it. You wish you were more like her: blonde hair, blue eyes, big boobs and all."

Asa stopped then, her face hardening into a scowl as she handed back the paper without another word. Turning away, she started walking home without him. He knew better than to catch up to her. Instead, he followed at a close distance until she was safely inside.

Chapter Five

A week passed, and Asa still hadn't spoken to him. Granted, he would never admit he missed her lectures and mean glances. And he refused to go to her house and groveled even though he actually considered it several times. Asa was playing with his head, and he refused to give in this time.

"You've been in a foul mood this past week," his mom informed as she handed him the bowl of pasta and shrimp.

"Have I," he said dismissively, taking a small portion of the food, knowing it would be horrible. He loved his mom, but the woman couldn't cook. "I didn't notice."

His dad smiled.

"Why don't you apologize for whatever you did?" Jackson Granger encouraged, tired of dealing with his mopey teenage son.

"I didn't do anything," Ian frowned and stared at his food.

"Okay, then why is she so mad at you?"

His father also studied the overcooked shrimp with disdain.

"Asa is weird," he proposed, shrugging his shoulders. "She got upset that Misty gave me her phone number."

"I see," Mr. Granger said, then took a small bite of his dinner then quickly washed it down with half a glass of water.

"How is it?" his mother, Ramona, asked nervously.

"Good," His father swallowed hard. "Do you like Misty?"

"No," Ian answered truthfully. "She's beautiful, no doubt, but she's shallow and mean."

"Did you tell Asa that?" His mother's blue eyes twinkled knowingly.

"No, but she's just as guilty as me," he clarified, hoping to mask his guilt.

"What did she do, son?" both adults questioned in unison.

"She *danced… with Brian… three* dances she danced with him."

His parents stared at him, then at each other, and smirked.

"Why are you looking at me like that?" he groaned.

Realizing his wife was distracted, his father covered his plate with a napkin like he was trying to bury his dinner.

"When are you going to admit you like her?"

"Who?" Ian gasped.

"Asa," his mother answered off-handedly, offering him another portion, and he grimaced.

"I only like her as a friend," he muttered unconvincingly.

"Uh huh," his dad chuckled, reaching for the bowl of salad, piling his plate high with the assortment of organic field greens, perfectly ripened tomatoes, and crisp cucumbers.

Thank goodness his mom could assemble a salad. Otherwise, they would have all starved to death years ago. If it wasn't for Mrs. Addams' amazing culinary skills, he'd definitely be stick thin.

"May I be excused?" he begged, pushing away his plate. "I'm not hungry."

"Sure," they both responded and then watched as their teenager trudged upstairs to his room.

Agitated and wide awake, Ian glanced at his bedside clock and then frowned. It was almost one in the morning, and he still couldn't sleep. Sadly, hunger pains gnawed at his gut while missing his best friend haunted his mind.

Unable to control his actions, he bounded from the bed and went to the window. Up above, the sky was clear, bright, and filled with stars. Deliberately, he glanced toward Asa's roof and was surprised to see her sitting wrapped in a blanket, staring overhead.

It took him less than a minute to grab his jacket and sneakers and slip out of the house. She didn't seem to notice as he climbed up the ladder until he cleared his throat.

"May I join you, or am I still in danger of being pushed off?"

Of course, there was no answer.

"I'm going to sit," he announced. "If you push me, my parents will sue."

To his relief, Asa laughed and patted the cushion beside her.

"I wouldn't want that," she joked playfully, continuing to watch the heavens.

"Couldn't sleep either?" he asked, noticing she was wearing only a thin football jersey and boy shorts that barely reached the top of her glorious thighs…

"Stop ogling me," she chastised without heat.

"You shouldn't wear stuff like that," he lectured, covering his lap with his jacket to hide his hardening member.

"I was going to bed," she admonished with a smirk.

"Well, it's not appropriate sleepwear," he added. "You'll catch a cold."

"Fine," she chuckled, adjusting the blanket to cover her entirely. "Why are you up so late?"

"I'm starving, and I couldn't sleep," he revealed as his growling stomach complained loudly.

That, of course, made her giggle, and the sound went straight to his groin. Not wanting her to see him in this condition, he discreetly adjusted himself to ease the ache.

"Did your mom make dinner again?" his friend successfully guessed.

He hung his head low.

"Wait here," Asa relayed. "I'll be right back."

"Where are you going?" His eyes went directly to her ass as she stood, and his errant member grew another painful inch.

No! Stop that!

"It's a surprise," she gave an innocent smile as she retreated through her window.

"While you're in there, grab your robe."

A few minutes later, she returned carrying several plastic containers, a fork, and a bottle of water. Thank goodness she was also wearing her robe.

"Here," she said, handing him the items.

Without hesitation, he opened the containers and grinned.

"Salisbury steak, mashed potatoes, and corn," Ian sighed.

Then like a man who hadn't eaten in days, he grabbed the fork and began shoveling food into his mouth, completely unaware of her disapproving stare.

Her best friend was acting like a caveman, Asa thought to herself, but she wasn't in the least bit surprised. *What girl in her right mind would want anything to do with him?*

Certainly not her.

Unfortunately, if that was the case, why was she being kept awake by erotic dreams staring at the young man inhaling leftovers beside her? Truthfully, she knew why. Ian was mesmerizing with his dark hair, hypnotic azure eyes, and the kind of face that inspired countries to go to war. And his body. Every inch of him was a sculpted masterpiece of lean, unyielding muscle.

As if reading her mind, he looked up, mouth chewing ravenously.

"What?"

"Nothing," she lied, trying to suppress her inappropriate thoughts. "Slow down before you choke."

Robotically, she handed him a napkin.

"Oh my gosh!" Ian moaned with unabashed delight. "This is so good."

"Better?" Asa rolled her eyes.

"Yes." he sighed as he finished the last bite. "Much better."

There was a brief pause.

"What do you want for your birthday next month?"

"Nothing," she fibbed again.

Was it inappropriate to say you?

"My parents are taking me to a new restaurant in town," she explained. "Mom's friend from culinary school owns it."

"Sounds like fun." He laughed when she made a funny face. "Tell me what you want so I don't end up buying you something you hate."

"You know what I like," she insisted, elbowing him gently on the arm. "Surprise me."

"If you hate my gift, I'm going to be pissed," he told, rubbing his nape in frustration.

"I won't hate your gift... I lo... I like anything." She faked a cough to distract him.

Wanting her near, he pulled her closer, and they snuggled on the blanket, staring up at the twinkling lights above. The early summer night was warm and comfortable. To his surprise, Asa arranged her head on his bicep as she allowed him to touch her hair. The soft, shiny tresses smelled of roses, her favorite fragrance.

"How's Misty?" she blurted out of the blue.

"How should I know," he blustered. It wasn't a question.

"I thought you would have called her already. It's been a whole week since she gave you her number. Aren't you excited...

to get to know her better?" she teased in her best Misty impression… which was pretty close to how Misty actually sounded.

"Listen to me closely, Asa," his tone harsher than intended. "I had no intention of calling her. I was caught off guard, and I didn't want to hurt her feelings, got it?"

"I got it." She shivered, and he pulled her closer, arranging the blanket more securely over both of them.

"I'm not attracted to Misty," he admitted, inhaling her fragrance.

Asa grinned but didn't respond.

"I just thought you should know."

It had been more than thirty minutes since Ian first arrived at Asa's place. He knew she had gone to the city for dinner at an exclusive restaurant, but she should have been back already. In the pit of his stomach, the normal-sized butterflies were now morphing into gigantic bats, and they were threatening to rip his intestines apart.

"Asa," Ian whispered. "Asa, where the hell are you?"

"I'm right here. Jeez!" she announced as she came around the side of the house.

Thirsty eyes instantly drank her in. She looked amazing wearing a pale-yellow sundress that reached the top of her knees, showcasing the long, elegantly shaped legs she had acquired during soccer practice. A simple pair of matching wedge sandals adorned her feet. Her long, silky locks were gathered in a low ponytail, and her make-up was expertly applied. Needless to say, she was breathtaking, and suddenly he felt an unusual tightening in his chest.

"You're late," he scolded, earning him an eye roll.

"The traffic from the city was heavy," she explained with an annoyed huff.

"C'mon," he said, taking her hand in his. "I've got a surprise for you."

Without argument, she followed him across the street to his house. Their houses were exactly the same except for the paint color. His was a light gray with deep burgundy and white trim. "Where are you taking me?"

"To my backyard," he replied, pulling her along beside him.

Asa had been to his house hundreds of times and knew the space was nondescript, to say the least. The Grangers led busy lives and didn't have much time for gardening, so their yard was just an empty grassy expanse, well-kept but boring. "What are we gonna do there?"

"You'll see," he ordered, then stopped abruptly. "Close your eyes."

"Why?" she countered.

"Just do it," he sighed, pleased when she followed his instructions. "Don't open them until I tell you to."

Silently, she waited, holding her breath in anticipation. After what seemed to be an eternity, Ian returned, taking her hand once again and guiding her across the yard.

"Can I open my eyes now?"

"Not yet," he pleaded, as the sound of something crackling caught her attention.

"Ian, where are we?"

"Okay," he said finally. "Open your eyes."

The scene laid out in front of her made her want to cry, but she didn't. She sniffled but refused to let the tears that were forming escape their confines.

"It's breathtaking," she complimented, sweeping the area with an appreciative glance.

Miraculously, Ian's once dreary backyard was now transformed into a lush and exotic retreat. There was a small fountain surrounded by newly planted flowers, an intricate stone patio area with a free-standing hammock, and a handmade fire pit that crackled and crunched as the flames rose toward the cloudless sky. Meticulously strung Christmas lights helped illuminate the cozy area giving it a soft romantic glow.

It truly did take her breath away.

Ian spoke first.

"Are you positive that you like it?"

"When did you do this?" she grinned gleefully, trying unsuccessfully to hide the emotion in her voice.

"I've been working on it for a couple of weeks," he grinned too. "My dad helped."

Looking down at his feet, he repeated, "You really like it?"

"I love it," she whispered, squeezing his hand. "I honestly do."

Releasing a pent-up breath, he maneuvered her lithe form toward the newly installed hammock.

"Sit down, please," Ian invited. "Don't move. I'll be right back."

Without another word, he disappeared into the house through the unlocked sliding glass door.

Elated by the transformation, Asa sat admiring the lovely space. It really was remarkable what he had done with the almost barren area. Ian never ceased to amaze her.

A moment later, he returned holding a familiar plastic storage container.

"What's that?" she beamed.

"Close your eyes and open your mouth," he requested.

She did as she was told, anxious for her additional surprise.

He placed something on her tongue. It was small, round, hard, and tasted sweet.

"Chocolate," she moaned as the flavor of raspberry-filled dark chocolate truffle coated her tongue.

"What do you think?" he questioned nervously.

"It's the best thing I've ever eaten!" she exclaimed without hesitancy. "Where did you buy it?"

"I didn't buy it," he blushed. "I made it."

"No. You. Did. Not," she gaped in surprise.

"I did," he claimed, popping one in his mouth as well. "Your mom let me borrow a few of her recipes, and I played around with the ingredients until I was satisfied with how it tasted. I know you love chocolate and raspberries. I guessed you'd like them together."

"Mmm," she moaned again, the sexy sound going straight to his cock. "Sit with me." Asa scooted over to make room for his much larger body on the hammock.

"I don't want it to break," he admitted bashfully.

His best friend chuckled.

"You're not that big." She paused. "That's not true. Your body is normal. It's your head that's too big. I think your huge ego stretched it out."

She'd never admit to him she thought he was the epitome of male beauty. All of the girls in their sophomore class last school year flirted and fawned all over him to the point where even he became uncomfortable. In her mind, she had to insult him to keep him grounded.

"Move over some more. You know, for someone only 5'4", 110 pounds soaking wet… you take up a lot of space," he taunted back.

Carefully, he maneuvered his six-foot frame into place beside her, relieved that the metal device holding the hammock above the earth creaked but didn't bow.

"Are you comfortable?"

"Uh-huh," she giggled, reaching across his chest to take another truffle from the container he still held. "Thank you."

"For what?" he grinned, startled by the way she was looking at him.

"For being so thoughtful," she smiled, revealing a small dimple on her left cheek. Surprisingly, he'd never noticed it before.

"I'm glad you like it," he sighed, unable to tear his eyes away from her soft, plump lips.

It was now or never. If she punched him, so be it. He was willing to take the chance. Slowly, he leaned forward, giving her the opportunity to pull away if she chose. To his delight, the raven-haired beauty leaned toward him.

With feather-light pressure, he brushed his lips against hers, astonished by the softness of her full lips. Holding her around the waist, Ian hauled her against his chest. Instinctively, his grip on her tightened as their bodies pressed firmly together. Gathering his courage, he pushed against her mouth with his tongue, seeking entrance. Hesitantly, she opened for him, allowing him access to the warm, moist space. Finding her tongue, he dueled with her, creating a rhythm that he felt in his groin. Immediately, he stopped when his cock hardened.

Asa, feeling the evidence of his arousal on her hip, halted too.

"Is that—"

"Sorry."

He tried to pull away, but she held him to her, ignoring his current state.

"Don't worry about it," she soothed. "You're a guy. A brand-new truck gets you horny."

"Yup," he agreed, wanting to kiss her again.

"How does it feel being sixteen?" Ian swiftly changed the subject.

"The same as fifteen," she inhaled deeply, resting her head on his bicep. The sweet scent of roses battered his senses.

He laughed.

"Why are you laughing?"

"You're a cougar," he snickered, knowing the comment would annoy her.

It didn't surprise him when she punched his shoulder hard.

"I am not a cougar," she reprimanded. "Your birthday is next month."

"I know," he chuckled. "But for the next three weeks, I have the satisfaction of knowing I was taken advantage of by an older woman."

His statement was rewarded with another punch to the arm, followed by a hard shove that sent him sprawling on the grass beside the hammock.

"Hey!" he laughed again, gazing up into sparkling brown eyes. "You could have killed me."

"Better to be shoved off of a hammock rather than a rooftop," she informed with a mischievous wink.

"Happy birthday, Asa."

He sat up and gave her a quick kiss on the forehead, and from his position sitting on the lush grass, he held her hand as they counted stars together.

Chapter Six

Two years later…

"Surprise!" the entire crowd shouted as Ian entered his parents' living room.

The space was packed to the brim with all of his favorite family members, close friends, and longtime neighbors. All of them smiling, laughing, and making small talk. Some he hadn't seen in months, others years. It shocked him that they all took time from their busy schedules to celebrate with him.

"Happy eighteenth birthday, Son," his father beamed, hugging him tightly.

"Thanks, Dad," he replied, struggling for breath.

"Congratulations on being accepted into the *CIA*," Brian patted his shoulder. "Hope you know how to shoot."

Ian chuckled.

He still couldn't believe it was true. For several years, he had longed to attend the famed culinary academy. Often, he would daydream of studying with famous chefs who preceded him, learning from the best, as it were. Now that he was formally accepted, he thought life couldn't get any better than this.

"It's the *Culinary Institute of America,* not the actual *CIA,*" he clarified, rolling his eyes. Then he scanned the crowded room. "Where's Asa?"

Brian snickered; hazel eyes filled with mirth.

"When are the two of you gonna get together?"

"I don't know what you're referring to," he lied, as was his custom when dealing with this particular subject.

"Everyone knows you've got it bad for her," Brian playfully ribbed. "Propose already and get it over with."

"What?!" Ian's face reddened.

"Marry her," his friend continued. "Have lots of sex and babies and give up this charade of being *only friends.*"

"It's not a charade," Ian smirked. "We are only friends."

"Great to know," Brian snickered. "Then you won't mind me asking her out."

"Ask her out, and I'll spray paint '*I'm a New England Patriots fan*' on the hood of your Jeep."

"You wouldn't!" Brian gasped in horror.

"Try me," he mimicked.

"Hold that thought." The other guy motioned to the foyer. "Your girl is here."

"She's *not* my girl." Ian stared mouth ajar, eyes sparkling with longing and lust.

"Whatever you say, man," Brian mocked, then walked away, leaving him to gawk at the goddess who had captured his heart years ago.

Asa looked stunning in a pair of black skinny jeans, a gold sequined top, a black blazer, and two-inch black heeled boots. Her shoulder-length ebony hair caressed the top of her shoulders with every nod of her head. Even the sway of her slim hips, as she walked toward him spoke to him on a primal level. Everything about her was sheer perfection.

"Happy birthday, Ian," Asa whispered near his ear, her soft tone startling him out of his love-induced haze.

"Thanks," he grinned.

"I didn't expect so many people," she said, glancing around nervously. "Anyway, how does it feel being the big one/eight?"

"The same as the big one/seven," he chuckled, happy to admire her beauty from such a close proximity. "I'm glad you could make it. Work let out early?"

Asa had been working part-time at an art gallery in the city on evenings and weekends. She worked for minimum wage but made up for it by being the owner's assistant on photo shoots. It thrilled her to be learning firsthand what it took to be a great photographer.

"It was a slow day, so Miriam said I could leave early. She knew I couldn't miss your big night."

"Ian," his mother called from the kitchen. "Come in here for a minute. I need some help."

Asa placed a hand at his elbow, stopping him.

"Go mingle with your guests," she encouraged. "Enjoy your night. I'll help your mom."

"Are you sure?"

"Yeah, I'd rather talk to your mom than make small talk with these characters," she chuckled.

"You're the best." He kissed her chastely at the side of the mouth.

The heated stare she gave him made him want to spontaneously combust. *What was that about?* The last time she looked at him like that, they were lying on his hammock, celebrating her sixteenth birthday with friendly banter and homemade chocolate truffles. The next thing he knew, they were kissing. It was the best kiss of his life.

"Hey, birthday boy," Misty keened as she wrapped her arms around his waist. "Hi, Asa," she added off-handedly.

Asa acknowledged her with a slight nod.

"I have something special planned for your birthday," the woman announced, turning back to him.

"Really?" he inquired, trying to unwind her arms from around his middle. "What is it?"

"I have to give it to you privately." Then she reached down and squeezed his ass right in front of his best friend. The low growl that escaped Asa's lips was thankfully drowned out by an upbeat Bruno Mars track. "Come with me."

"Where are we going?"

"To my SUV," she giggled. "I need some help with my *battery*."

That was Asa's cue. Without a word, she turned and stormed toward the kitchen, never once glancing back. However, he knew that posture and was sure he'd pay for Misty's unwarranted advances later.

"I don't think that's a good idea," he stated firmly when Asa was out of earshot. "I don't like you that way."

"I know you're attracted to me; admit it," the overly flirtatious female cooed, then kissed his chin. "I've seen the way you look at me. Plus, I've already had you."

"That was a mistake," Ian's voice lowered as he looked around guiltily.

"You didn't seem to think so while your tongue was buried in my p—"

Filled with remorse, he shook his head, heat flooding his cheeks.

"You're beautiful, no doubt, but... but I—"

"You're in love with Asa," she snarled.

"Y-yes… no… I don't know," he stammered like a gibbering fool.

"If you change your mind," Misty replied with a mock pout, giving him another kiss to the chin. "You know where to find me."

To his dismay, Asa was scarce for the rest of the party. Only appearing occasionally to help clean up, refill empty food containers, and chat with a handful of friends. Other than that, she stayed in the kitchen with his mom. She disappeared completely when it was time to cut the birthday cake Mrs. Addams made for the occasion.

"Where is Asa?" he asked Brian, who was eagerly awaiting a slice of the delectable double chocolate confection. "I haven't seen her in a while."

"I helped her take some dishes back to her house," Brian eyed the cake longingly. "I think she went back home."

"I'm not surprised," he said emotionlessly, trying to hide his disappointment.

"What did you do to piss her off now?"

"Nothing," he frowned, cutting through the three layers of the professionally decorated cake. "Well… Misty tried to—"

"Say no more," his friend chuckled. "Whenever Misty is around, Asa escapes."

"I don't know what happened between the two of them." He sliced the cake equally and distributed the pieces onto festive paper plates.

"Asa never told you?" Brian's eyes narrowed suspiciously.

"If you haven't noticed, Asa isn't exactly a chatterbox. I have to practically pry small bits of information from her, and it has to be done carefully in order to not arouse suspicion."

"Is she a woman or a field operative?"

"She's a little of both." Ian smiled. "That's why I like her. She's a Rubik's Cube, hard to figure out."

The party was a complete success until his best friend flew the coop. Now, it was his job to make sure she was still speaking to him. It was a fifty-fifty chance.

"Asa," Ian yelled from below her bedroom window.

With great force, she threw open her window.

"Go away!" the headstrong vixen yelled. "I don't want to talk to you!"

"Don't be stubborn!" he admonished.

"Don't you have to shower?"

"Why would I need to take a shower?" His brow wrinkled with confusion. "I took one earlier this evening before the party."

"You need to wash away the scent of that harlot on you," the woman hissed.

Realization suddenly dawned.

"I didn't have sex with Misty."

"Liar," she hissed again and gave him a feral grin that made his balls draw up tight.

"I'm telling the truth," he sighed, continuing to stare up at her.

"I don't believe you," Asa started to close the window.

"Wait!" Ian begged. "Come down here and smell me if you don't believe me."

"No," she snarled. "You could have taken a shower and put back on the same clothes."

"You're being ridiculous." His temper flared as he watched her watching him, the gears in her mind grinding. "C'mon," he urged. "I brought dessert."

He knew that would get her. Asa loved sweets.

Contemplating his words, she finally conceded.

"I'll be right down," she agreed. "But it's not because of you. I only want dessert."

As promised, a few moments later, she opened the door, hair messy, wearing her favorite football jersey and the boy shorts he often dreamed of.

"Why are you not properly clothed?" he asked, willing his misbehaving member to go back to sleep.

"I am properly clothed," she responded as she glanced down at her outfit. "I was sleeping."

"I can see your... your—" His mouth went dry, and his tongue felt like it weighed a ton.

Looking down, she saw what he was staring at. Her shirt was so worn he could see the outline of her dark areolas through the material. A shocked gasp pulled from her throat.

"Crap!"

Swiftly, Asa ran back inside and returned shortly wearing a fluffy, blue terry cloth robe that hit her long, slender legs at the knees.

"Is this better?" Her cheeks heated.

"Much," he sighed, still seeing those tempting mounds in his mind. "I hope we're not being too loud. I wouldn't want to wake your parents."

"They're not here," she informed. "They went to Seattle for some kind of weather convention."

"Really," he said, his mind suddenly going blank. "Here, this is for you."

"It's a slice of your birthday cake." Asa's features softened.

"I know how much you love chocolate," he reminded sheepishly.

She smiled at the container and then at him.

"Do you want to share it?"

He nodded. In actuality, he would eat the entire slice if she'd let him.

"Come in."

Chapter Seven

Dessert always did the trick. Asa quickly forgave him and shared the slice of chocolate rapture. Without it as an offering, he would have surely been a corpse.

"This should be illegal," Ian hummed, licking the tines of his fork.

"I agree." Asa's actions mimicked his. "My mother is an amazing cook."

"I've said it before and I'll say it again," he leaned back in his chair and patted his stomach, "… if your parents ever get divorced—"

"I know, you'd marry my mom," she grimaced.

"Got that right," he chuckled, earning him a playful slap to the hand then he glanced at the kitchen clock. "It's late. I better get going."

"Wait, I haven't given you your present." She motioned for him to follow her outside. "Close your eyes."

He did.

"Don't open them until I tell you."

"Okay," he snickered as she took his hand and led him to the back door.

"Step down," she ordered. "Stay right there. Keep your eyes closed."

Next, he heard paper rustling and something being pulled across the stone floor of the patio.

"Are you ready?"

"Yes," he answered anxiously. "Hurry up! I'm opening my eyes."

"Go ahead," she encouraged. "Open them."

In front of him stood a large easel with a huge, framed collage of pictures, all pictures of *them*. Expertly arranged photographs starting at the age of five intermingled with candid shots of him at his birthday party a few hours ago.

"How long did it take to assemble this?" he questioned in awe of the amazing gift.

"A few months," Asa beamed. "I had to find all of the pictures, buy the supplies, and organize everything perfectly. I also built the frame. That's why I left the party early. I had to develop the ones I took tonight and position them with the rest of the photographs."

"No, you didn't do this by yourself," he gasped, admiring the quality of the final product. Asa's eye for detail couldn't be ignored.

"You like it then?" She fiddled with the pocket of her robe. "If you don't like it I could—"

"I love it," he whispered. "It's us, *together*. What wouldn't I like about that?" He stepped closer, taking her hand in his, when she tried to pull it away, he held it tighter. "Thank you."

"You're welcome," she blushed, took a step back, and tripped over one of her mom's potted herbs.

Surprisingly, he lunged forward, grabbed her around the waist, and saved her from landing against the hard stone surface. Without permission, he kissed her, shocked when she kissed him back. Slender arms gripping his shoulders like they were the only thing tethering her to the Earth.

"You make me crazy," he sighed longingly, finally pulling away an inch. The look in his azure gaze told her he wasn't joking.

"That sounds like a line," she smirked. "Are you trying to get inside my pants, Mr. Granger?"

"That was my intention, yes," his words muffled due to him burying his face against the side of her neck to inhale her unique fragrance. "We've got chemistry. Admit it."

"We don't," she denied, trying to fortify her weakening defenses.

"Stubborn," he chuckled, tracing a line from her earlobe to her collarbone with his tongue. "Why do I like you so much when all you do is push me away?"

"You must be a glutton for punishment," she answered with all seriousness. "I'm leaving."

Pulling away a few inches, he glared at her.

"What do you mean, *leaving*? Now, in the middle of our negotiation?" he waggled his brows playfully.

"No," her voice lowered to barely a whisper. "I mean, I'm leaving the country."

He really did pull away from her then.

Several times, Asa mentioned wanting to see the world. Although it was few and far between, his best friend would go on rants about how one day she would stand in the middle of the Amazon Rainforest and take photographs of rare Brazilian songbirds or be on safari in the Serengeti observing a pride of lions lounging under a shady tree. It was a dream of hers, but he just couldn't wrap his mind around her not being close by.

"I don't understand. Where are you going?" he queried, helping her stand.

"The owner of the gallery invited me to be her assistant on a yearlong assignment for *National Geographic*. I'd travel the world with her, helping her collect shots for her monthly articles. Isn't that incredible?"

"Yeah," he grumbled half-heartedly. "But where does that leave us?"

"We're not a couple, Ian," Asa blinked back a tear. "We're just friends."

"Best friends," he reminded.

"Yes, of course... *best friends*," she solidified. "But you're leaving me anyway at the end of the summer to go to culinary school in New York, remember?"

That was also true. He already had housing for the fall semester and was looking forward to being on his own. Ian loved his parents, but he wanted to spread his wings and experience life on his own. He guessed Asa felt the same.

"I remember," he sighed solemnly. "I thought you'd—"

"You thought I'd be here waiting for you to come home, pining away, crying every night."

When he didn't respond, she sat on the soft grass carpet of her parent's backyard, looking up at his betrayed expression. She would never admit she'd be doing that anyway, regardless of where she was, but the opportunity to learn from a world-renowned photographer was too great an opportunity to pass up.

"What about art school?" Ian scowled.

"I've already spoken to a counselor at The Art Institute of Colorado, and they are going to hold my spot while I'm away. I can start when I return to the States."

Everything had fallen into place. Her travel visa and passport were expedited with the help of one of her father's college friends, who now was a bigwig in the federal government. Thrilled with Asa's travel opportunity, her pediatrician squeezed her in for a required physical and vaccinations even though her office was booked solid for over two months. Reluctantly, her parents agreed, which made her even more certain that it was her destiny to go on this adventure.

If only Ian could accept it.

"It sounds like you've got everything figured out," he grunted, turning to leave.

"Where are you going?" she asked, stunned by his reaction.

"Back home," he sighed again, his face etched with some unknown emotion.

"We're in the middle of a conversation!" she growled, upset he would retreat so easily.

"I guess I'm taking a play from the Asa Addams playbook of how to avoid intimacy."

"That's not fair!" the furious woman hissed, feeling the sting of his words.

"No, it's not," he agreed, anger flooding his entire nervous system. "It's not fair for me to feel so possessive of you or for us to be separated for an entire year."

"What are you talking about?!" she barked, throwing her arms above her head in exasperation.

"Nothing," he mumbled below his breath, carefully picked up his framed collage, and headed around the side of the house, leaving Asa bewildered and stunned.

An hour or so later, the sounds of muffled music tickled Asa's ears, waking her from a fitful slumber.

"Who the hell is playing music at..." she rubbed her eyes, trying to get them to focus on the digital alarm clock on her nightstand, "... three thirty-five in the morning?"

Angrily, she leaped out of bed, jogged to the slightly opened window, and yanked it wide. The sound was loud now, familiar, and coming from several feet below her window. Looking down, her eyes widened at the sight on her back lawn.

She grinned, unable to do anything else as Ian stood wearing his dad's trench coat and holding up his iPod, a steal-your-heart-grin plastered on his much too irresistible face.

"Turn that off, Ian!" she commanded, but he turned it up instead. "What are you doing, madman?"

"I saw it in a John Cusack movie," he grinned. "We watched it together a few years back."

"That's so cliché," Asa stifled an amused chuckle.

"It may be cliché, but it's effective," he laughed.

"You're a lunatic," she accused with a hostile glare.

"Probably." He stood gazing up at her with a huge smirk, daring her to come down and silence him. "What was the name of that movie?"

"' Say Anything,'" she educated with a scowl of epic proportions. "You're gonna wake the neighbors."

"We only have two other neighbors," he reminded cheekily. "Mrs. Carpenter is completely deaf when she takes off her hearing aid."

And he should know. Many times he had climbed Mrs. Carpenter's pear tree. Of course, Ian knew it was wrong, but every year the delicious fruit would call his name. In his defense, in order to make up for it, he would bake a pear tart for his unsuspecting neighbor, and if he didn't pick those pears, they would fall and rot.

"Mr. Peterson and his wife aren't deaf," she glared angrily, trying to keep a straight face. "Turn that damn thing off and go home."

"Not until you come down here and talk to me," he beseeched, refusing to leave.

"No," she contradicted stubbornly. "You're the one who walked away."

"It was a stupid thing to do," Ian shamefully admitted.

"You've got that right," Asa reprimanded, her temper softening.

"Forgive me?" he begged.

"No," she responded, then began closing the window.

Why did the woman have to be so damn difficult? His mind started swirling, running through what to do next. It was just his luck that she would leave the country and not have any contact with him for the year. Not this time. Oh, no! He wouldn't let their longtime friendship end this way.

"Then I'm turning up the volume," he boldly informed, praying that no one would call the police.

Good grief!

"No!"

"I'm reaching for the volume button right now… my fingers are touching it… it's getting louder… old Mr. Peterson is gonna call the cops—"

"Ok, fine… I'll be right out." Grabbing her robe, she ran downstairs, through the house, out the backdoor to the backyard where her best friend stood defiantly, blue eyes sparkling roguishly.

"Turn that off immediately," she pleaded, face flushed from her brisk jog as well as her growing embarrassment.

Ian continued his task, completely ignoring his highly agitated friend. When she came within arm's length, he grabbed her and pulled her against him, holding her immobile against his much stronger body. After a few seconds, she stopped struggling and allowed him to hold her.

Finally, he turned down the volume and, to her amazement, began to slow dance with her. The fading scent of his cologne lulled her into a false sense of security; he was up to something. She knew him too well.

"What are you doing?" she interrogated suspiciously.

"Continuing our negotiations," the need in his voice unchecked, raspy, and sexy.

"' *Lately, I've been, I've been losing sleep, Dreaming about the things that we could be,'*" Ian sang along to the song slithering through the small electronic device, continuing to hold her close.

Their bodies rubbing together made her dizzy with want, but she definitely wasn't going to tell him that. Ian already had Misty throwing herself at him, and she was sure there were others. No way! She had no intention of becoming one of Ian Granger's groupies.

"Isn't this 'Counting Stars' by 'One Republic'?" she giggled, enjoying his sultry singing voice. "I love this song."

Asa so rarely giggled he felt gifted by the small show of normality.

"Yeah," he admitted. "I'm not romantic enough to come up with something that would sweep you off of your feet, but this song reminds me of us."

"Spoken like a true romantic," she joked as she kissed the side of his neck. "What am I going to do with you?"

With shaky hands, she unbuttoned the top button of his shirt and placed a lingering kiss to the smooth skin beneath.

Shamelessly, he angled her head with the palm of his hand, so he could stare into her expressive eyes.

"Anything you want," he said as his lips met hers.

"Hmm," she moaned against his mouth, enjoying the slight scraping of his five o'clock shadow against her face and chin. The minor pain hitched up her desire another notch. "I've never done this before."

"We've kissed before," he laughed as he reminded. "Was it that forgettable?"

"I didn't mean it like that," she bristled. "I mean, I've never *negotiated.*"

"I know. What man in his right mind would have the balls to try *negotiations* with you?" he sighed, trying to lighten the mood.

"Have you?"

He was silent.

"Oh," she whispered, turning away. "Do I want to know with whom?"

Unfortunately, her only answer was the gentle breeze blowing through the treetops.

"Misty."

It wasn't a question, and the guilty look on his gorgeous face said it all.

"Please don't hold it against me." He held her hands, rubbing his thumbs along her wrists. "It happened last summer. I was horny, and we weren't talking, and she offered—"

"Stop." Her eyes welled with tears. "I don't need the play-by-play. I get the gist of it."

"It meant nothing," he placated, hoping it would redeem him somehow.

"Well, you can't change the past," she sighed. "I'm a little hurt. Why couldn't it have been someone else, anyone else? Why did you give something so valuable to *her*?"

"I'm an idiot," he confessed, making her smile.

Pulling out of his embrace, she announced, "Yes, you are an idiot."

Asa turned quickly to leave.

"Where are you going?" he questioned her, retreating back, a stunned expression on his face. In true Asa Addams form, she continued her withdrawal toward the dimly lit house, completely ignoring his desperate state.

"Asa?" he huffed at a moderate volume, trying not to wake the few neighbors they had.

His heart clenched in his chest.

"Damn it!" Ian swore. "If you're expecting me to chase after you..."

He paused, contemplating his next words carefully.

"You're wrong."

Shit!

Wordlessly, she walked into the house, leaving him staring after her, mouth agape, eyes wide. He stood looking at the back door until the light switched off. "Great," he mumbled sarcastically to himself. As he turned to leave, Asa's melodious voice halted his exit.

"Aren't you joining me?" she asked, holding the floral comforter from her bed tight against her chest.

He swallowed hard before asking.

"Is that a metaphor for something else?"

Please say yes... please say yes!

"If I have to ask twice, I'm rescinding my offer," she snickered.

Obediently, Ian followed her to the middle of the yard, underneath the tall oak tree that stood proudly in the middle of the grassy area. Patiently, he waited as she laid the comforter on the ground and motioned for him to join her when she sat. His heartbeat raced, and he prayed she wouldn't hear it over his amplified breathing.

Efficiently, she divested him of his shirt as her eyes roamed his naked upper body. A pleased smile appeared on her delectable lips. Leaning against the rough surface of the tree trunk, he watched with mesmerized eyes as Asa gracefully straddled his lap, their groins fitting perfectly against each other. Without a word, she brushed her lips against his, teasing him with light flicks of her tongue and barely-there caresses.

When he thought she'd never get the show on the road, she surprised him again by pulling away and eased the soft terry cloth robe from her toned shoulders, allowing it to land on his outstretched legs. He held his breath in anticipation as she leisurely removed the thin night shirt revealing two perky orbs to his grateful gaze.

Then quite bravely, she took both his hands and placed them against her heaving chest. They were perfect... not too big, but definitely more than a handful. He caressed her *there*, enjoying the soft, perfect globes and the erotic purrs and moans escaping her parted lips.

Leaning forward yet again, she took possession of his mouth. This time her kisses were demanding and brazen, and zealous. She consumed all of him: his mind, his heart, his body... with aggressive licks and mind-blowing nips to his mouth and tongue. His entire body heated under her insistent touches. There was no doubt Asa was the sun, and he was in orbit around her.

When he thought he'd explode, she pulled away, this time scooting back on his lap just enough to unbutton his jeans and lower the zipper. *Holy shit! This was really happening.* Impatiently, she tugged down the unwanted denim and cotton boxer brief in one sure movement. Her eyes enlarged as she stared at his more than impressive erection.

Smirking, she grabbed his rock-hard member at the base with both hands, leaned forward, and enclosed the mushroom-shaped head between her lips. Enthusiastically, she gorged on the swollen head like she was sucking a lollipop while her adventuresome tongue swirled around the tip tracing each contour and crevice, making him squirm.

Instinctively, he gathered her shoulder-length hair away from her face, so he could get a better view of her devouring his cock.

Asa blew his mind with every nip, every lick, every pull on his member, and he had to think of the *Denver Broncos* losing the *Super Bowl* in order not to blow his load right then and there. When his body stiffened, announcing his impending release, she stopped and reclaimed his already kiss-swollen lips. Thankfully, he regained his control. He'd never forgive himself if he finished before she did.

He wanted her naked. He needed her naked.

Unable to think rationally, he grabbed the silky black panties she wore and, with both hands, rendered them in two, tearing the fabric like it was a sheet of paper. The surprised gasp that escaped her encouraged him to continue. He hoped those weren't her favorite pair of panties. *Oh well.* He'd buy her an entire new wardrobe if she wanted him to at this point.

Asa's movements stilled as he maneuvered her drenched entrance over the engorged head of his cock. The warning in her dark orbs reminded him that he wasn't wearing protection. He would love, *love* to take her bareback, but that would be a foolish thing to do, all things considering.

She was leaving the country, and he would be going to the CIA at the end of the summer, and realistically he had no means of supporting a family if Asa got pregnant. Even though Asa carrying his child was an idea that actually made him smile.

Reaching inside his pocket, he retrieved his wallet. Hidden inside were a few *Trojans* he kept just in case of emergencies like this one. Honestly, he'd never had this type of emergency except for Misty, but he was glad that he was prepared.

One perfectly shaped eyebrow hitched to almost her hairline as she glared at him, and he felt his face redden immediately. A nervous snicker fell past his lips.

Tearing open the foil packet with his teeth, he sheathed his member in two efficient glides. Smiling as the extra-large condom barely contained all of his manhood. He chuckled as she rolled her eyes at his silent brag concerning the size of his cock.

Naughtily, she bent and nipped his earlobe, making him jump. Laughing wickedly, he cupped her flushed face in his hands and sealed their mouths together. Asa lost no time as she rose to her knees to get the proper height, reached back, took hold of him, and lined up his latex-covered member to her sopping-wet sex.

Holding off the urge to ram himself inside her and claim her like a beast in rut, Ian carefully pushed forward, lodging the thick head inside of her by only a few inches. Her body immediately became rigid as panic set in. Leaning forward, he covered one aching nipple with his lips, lavishing the beaded point with languid swipes with his tongue. She moaned, arching her back, wordlessly ordering him to take more of her. Excitedly, he engulfed her entire areola inside of his mouth, suckling possessively.

With his free hand, he found the swollen bud at the apex of her thighs, coated his finger in her cream, and began to gently rub the needy nub. Asa purred at his ministrations, and another trickle of arousal coated his shaft. The additional lubrication allowed him to push in a bit more; his movement halted by her maidenhead.

Nervously, he froze, waiting for her to ask him to stop, but as usual, she amazed him by pushing down onto his stiff member, breaking through the barrier. She winced, making him feel guilty for feeling such happiness when she felt uncomfortable. Gradually, she began to rise and fall upon his thickening appendage, moaning and writhing and driving him crazy with yearning. He met her thrust for thrust, letting her set the pace enjoying every movement she made.

As the need to come took hold of him, he roughly grabbed her rounded hips with such force he thought he'd bruised her, but her breathy sigh told him she didn't mind. Her head descended again, kissing him with such fervor he almost forgot his own name.

Who would have believed his reserved Asa would be such a hellion in the throes of passion?

Diligently, she worked him into a sexual frenzy. Their bodies slid against each other from the thin sheen of perspiration that coated them both while loud wet sounds as skin rubbing against skin infiltrated his senses, and persistent lips found those delicious spots that made them forget they were making love outside where anyone who happened to wander into the backyard would get an eyeful.

Then without warning, the tingling at the base of his spine, along with the sensation of his balls drawing up tight, was the signal he hovered at the edge of release. Quickening his thrusts, he consumed her mouth with desperation. At last, Asa's body stiffened, and her eyes closed as she threw her head back and gasped when the orgasm slammed into her. Clenching inner muscles gripped his cock like a vice and wrenched every drop of seed from his thrusting member into the latex barrier. A loud animalistic growl flew past his lips, the sound resembling some unholy creature that had escaped from the bowels of Hades.

Harsh ragged breaths caressed his well-defined chest as Asa's pliant body slumped against him, trying to calm her erratic breathing. Tenderly, he smoothed the stray strands of hair away from her flushed face and kissed her on the forehead as he touched her back with tender lingering strokes.

"I never thought you'd be such a wildcat," Ian chuckled.

She laughed and then pinched his nipple.

"I'm going to have to call you that from now on," he teased. "Wildcat."

"Don't you dare," she giggled, the innocent sound making his member harden again. "You can't be serious?"

Brown eyes narrowed suspiciously as his reawakened member currently poked her in the abdomen.

"What can I say?" he snorted. "The damn thing has a mind of its own."

She was quiet for a long time before finally speaking.

"Happy birthday, Ian," Asa whispered, her words accompanied by several wet kisses to his bare chest.

Squeezing her gently, he whispered back, "I'll treasure this gift, *always.*"

And he would.

Chapter Eight

Denver International Airport was a bustling hub, even at ten o'clock on a Thursday night. All around was the sound of luggage wheels rolling over polished tiles, people noisily debating whether to go directly to their gate or find somewhere to grab a quick bite before boarding, babies crying and a slew of other exciting spectacles. Asa couldn't help smiling, even though her parents were clearly freaking out, and Ian's worried expression was evident. None of it unnerved or diluted her excitement.

"Don't forget to call when you get to Morocco." Mr. Addams hugged his daughter for the third time in less than ten minutes.

"I will, Dad," she replied, hugging him back.

"And remember to carry your water bottle wherever you go," her mom reminded, sniffling as she smoothed back Asa's hair. "Be careful, and don't go wandering off alone. Also, don't forget about applying sunscreen whenever you're outside. You have a tendency to burn, and make sure you bring us back souvenirs."

"I won't forget," she said, smiling at her parents' obvious overreacting, secretly thrilled they would miss her so much. "I better get going. My flight will be boarding soon."

"I love you." Mrs. Addams hugged her one last time.

"Hope you have lots of fun," her dad added as he kissed her cheek.

"I will." Then she turned to Ian, who was watching her with a curious gaze. "You better miss me too."

"Don't worry; I will. You can count on it," he tried to smile but couldn't. "I'll be expecting lots of postcards and letters and emails and *whatever*."

He reached out to touch her cheek but stilled as her parents studied them knowingly.

"Don't hook up with any Bedouin tribe leaders," he teased.

"Don't burn down the CIA," she teased back, eyes filling with unshed tears making him want to touch her even more.

Suddenly, she hugged him. The soft fragrance of roses filled his senses and embedded into his soul.

"I'm serious," Ian expressed seriously. "Call me when you get to your hotel."

"I promise. *Wow* them at culinary school," she encouraged, squeezing him tighter. "I better go before I change my mind."

"Okay," he agreed, kissing her cheek and then releasing her.

All three watched as she jogged to the counter, gave her boarding pass to the attendant, and then turned back one last time to wave before disappearing down the corridor leading to the awaiting 747. His chest tightened at the realization he wouldn't see her for an entire year or more, depending on his breaks.

"Don't look so glum," Mr. Addams encouraged, clapping him on the shoulder. "She'll be back before we know it."

"C'mon, I've got fresh-baked cookies waiting for us at the house," Mrs. Addams announced as she wiped her tears with a tissue.

Damn it!

Not even the legendary chocolate chip cookies could raise his deflated spirit. The thought of eating them made his stomach roil. He sighed. Now he knew for sure he was in love with her.

Looking around the small yet elegantly furnished hotel room, Asa sighed. She'd never been this far away from home before, and it was a tad scarier than she imagined. Since she was a little girl, her family would travel, so her mother and father always accompanied her. This time she had her boss, but it wasn't quite the same. It was also the first time she had an entire hotel room to herself.

Then it happened. Anxiety flooded her thoughts as images of Ian saying goodbye to her at the airport bombarded her. Needing to hear his voice, she picked up the phone and dialed zero for the hotel's operator.

A few seconds later, a feminine voice answered.

"Bonjour! This is Marie. How may I assist you?" The strong French accent was difficult to understand.

"H-hello," she stammered. "I'm trying to get an outside line to make a long-distance call to the United States."

The operator good-naturedly explained the process.

"Thank you, Marie."

As she dialed Ian's cell phone, she waited on pins and needles. Thank goodness he picked up on the third ring.

"Missed me already?" he ribbed.

"No," she fibbed, knowing he couldn't see how much his voice calmed her.

"I missed you as soon as you boarded the plane," his voice lowered to that seductive timbre that she loved.

"Did you?" she giggled, relaxing more.

"How long will you be in Morocco?"

Wanting to be accurate, Asa found her itinerary and gave it a quick scan. Miriam, her mentor, and supervisor, had a packed schedule: excursions to the desert, camel rides, several trips to the local bazaar, not to mention visiting Miriam's local friends. It was going to be wonderful!

"Almost a week," she informed, taking off her shoes and sitting cross-legged on the comfortable mattress of the twin-sized bed.

"How was the flight?"

"It was good, very little turbulence," Asa beamed. "We changed planes in London, but I slept for most of the trip."

"Have you eaten yet?" his concern was unnecessary but welcomed.

"We ate at a fancy restaurant across the street," she admitted as she ran her left palm over the ridiculously soft material. "It was delicious."

"And…"

"And, *what*?" she feigned ignorance, knowing what he wanted her to do next.

"Tell me," he coerced with a lighthearted tone.

"You're a lunatic," she chuckled, her remaining tension seeping away.

"I know, but you're gonna do it anyway," he convinced with an audible smile in his voice.

"All right," she laid on the mattress, legs crossed at the ankles, one arm holding the phone to her ear, the other hand resting on her stomach. "Are you ready?"

"Believe me, I was born ready," he answered in a low tone that made her toes curl.

"I'm no good at this," she blushed, closing her eyes.

"Try it anyway, for me," the insufferable flirt added.

"Ok, here goes." Clearing her throat, she began. "First, I had a crisp organic field green salad with a light yet flavorful citrus vinaigrette. The second course was a vegetable soup with lots of julienned leeks and potatoes—"

"Hold it!" he implored enthusiastically. "Use more descriptive words and speak slowly."

She grinned to herself.

What other man would get so wound up over food?

At last, Asa continued.

"The main course was a hearty lamb and root vegetable stew over a bed of wild rice…."

Chapter Nine

A little over a year later…

"When is Asa coming back?" Brian prodded right before taking a large bite of his bacon double cheeseburger.

"I'm not sure," Ian replied, took a sip of his drink, and then swallowed the lump in his throat. "I got a postcard from her last month from Manaus, Brazil, but since then, she's been stuck in Central America because of mudslides and washed-out roads used to access where she's staying."

"That's amazing," Brian beamed. "She's been all over the world. I wonder if she'll be the same old Asa."

"Hopefully," he sighed after taking another gulp of his cola.

The past year had been stressful but fun. Ian loved training to be a chef. He enjoyed creating menus, learning how to butcher meat, meeting celebrity chefs who graduated from the *Institute*, experimenting with dry rubs, producing self-created marinades, and everything else that went into his field. He had cool roommates, too, and Hyde Park was a beautiful area filled with historic houses, museums, and quaint shops and restaurants.

What it didn't have was Asa.

His long-time friend stopped in mid-bite and stared at him.

"Are you going to tell her?"

"If it comes up," Ian revealed anxiously, taking a French fry and shoving it into his mouth.

"How is it not going to come up?" his childhood friend commented with an accusatory tone. "You can't let her find out on her own. She'll really kill you then."

"Why are you hounding me with all of these questions?!" Ian snapped, then apologized.

"I'll drop it if you want me to, but you need to tell her A.S.A.P. unless you want to completely ruin your friendship," Brian reprimanded as he reached for the ketchup.

"Shut up," he growled, knowing the other man was right. "When the opportunity presents itself, I'll tell her, okay?"

"Okay," Brian acknowledged, then took another bite of his burger.

The sound of music filtered through his window, waking him from a dead sleep. Rubbing his eyes, he glanced at his bedside clock… two o'clock in the morning. He was going to kick the ass of whoever was playing their music this loud so early. In a sleep-induced haze, he plodded to the window and looked outside for the offending culprit.

Finally, his eyes focused on a blurry shape across the street perched on the Addams' roof. When the form came into focus, he almost tripped over his own feet as he ran from his bedroom, through his house, across the desolate street, toward his best friend's dwelling. The ladder was where it always was, leaning against the side of the house. Carefully, he climbed up, and thankfully, his adrenaline overwhelmed his fear of heights.

"You're back!" he whimpered at the sight of Asa smiling sweetly at him, her hair much longer now and hanging loosely to the middle of her back. She had lost a little weight, which worried him, but she still looked healthy and happy. For some reason, she seemed different, more mature. She'd always acted older than she was, but now she radiated sophistication. He rubbed his palm over his aching heart to subdue the sensation.

"I am," she smiled, her hand outstretched, waiting for him to join her.

"You're going to wake the neighbors," he taunted playfully. "Or at least the ones who aren't hard of hearing."

"Oh well," she replied, shrugging her shoulders. "I'll apologize with my mom's cookies tomorrow."

As always, her smile took his breath away. For the last thirteen months, he'd fantasized about their reunion. Ian had vividly imagined their passionate embraces, long, adventurous caresses, and a really hot make-out session leading into really hot sex, but the reality of the scene was quite different.

They were different.

Clearing his throat to ease his nervousness, he agreed.

"That usually works wonders," he grinned. "Those cookies have gotten us out of many a problem."

"Sit with me," Asa beckoned, and as soon as he sat, she hugged him tightly. The recognizable scent of her rose shampoo made him feel guilty. No. It made him feel sad. Sad for what he now had to do.

"Tell me everything starting from the moment you boarded your flight," he requested, stalling for time.

"Before we get caught up," she took something out of her backpack. "This is for you." She handed him a small bundle of handwritten...

"Recipes?" His heart really did feel heavy then.

"Whenever I ate something amazing, I thought of you," she smiled broadly. "I used my considerable *charm* to get the recipes from various chefs and home cooks that I met on my trek around the world. I knew you'd love them."

Guilt-ridden, he sat silently, staring down at the thoughtful gift.

"I'm such a bastard," he mumbled under his breath.

"What did you say?" Asa queried, dark eyes glistening under the starry skies.

"Nothing," he smiled, but her eyes narrowed curiously.

"Aren't you glad to see me?" she pouted, resting her hand on his.

"Of course I am," Ian glowed. "I've missed you so much I can't even express how much."

"Then kiss me," she requested, leaning forward, waiting for his touch. When he didn't comply, she huffed. "Now I know something is wrong."

Ian opened his mouth to say something, but he stopped before he got the words out.

"Whatever it is, it can't be that bad?" she jibed.

The whisper of the night air through the boughs of the oak tree was the only response.

"You flunked out of culinary school!" she gasped.

He shook his head.

"Umm… you're getting a sex change?" she joked, and the pained expression on his face made her smile disappear. "What is it?"

"Misty—"

"What about Misty?" she frowned, face hardening.

"She thinks she's pregnant," his voice barely perceptible.

"I'm not surprised," Asa scoffed. "Are you?"

Slowly, he nodded his answer.

"Why would Misty being pregnant have you so—" The realization slammed into her as she sucked in a shuddering breath, and tears instantly began to stream down her face. Silently, she stood and made her way to the awaiting ladder.

"Come back here," he pleaded against the silence battering his ears. "Asa, please let me explain."

Carelessly, she whipped around, her body near the edge, making him concerned for her safety.

"What would you like to explain? How you did it? Where you did it? How many times you did do it? You selfish motherfucker!" her voice rose to an unbelievable shriek filled with anger and betrayal. "Do you remember what you told me?"

He shook his head.

"You told me not to hook up with anyone overseas," Asa reminded. "Apparently, you were joking, or it only applied to me. Stupid me, I took it as *I'll wait for you.*"

Wanting to calm her, Ian stood to follow and tried not to think of where they were arguing.

"I didn't mean for it to happen," he blurted, which earned him a huge scowl.

"No, really?" she hissed facetiously. "What happened? Did you trip, fall, and land in her vagina?"

She almost choked on the words.

"My god!" Asa bellowed. "Why didn't you wear a condom?"

"Damn it! I did," he yelled back, scrubbing his hands over his face in a sign of frustration.

Suddenly Asa stopped moving and turned back to glare at him.

"Then how is she pregnant?"

"It must have broken," Ian mumbled. "I'm as shocked as you are."

"You know what would have been a foolproof way to prevent her from getting pregnant?" his best friend sniffled.

"What?"

"Not sticking your fucking dick inside of her, to begin with."

Her entire body was shaking now, and it took all of his self-control not to reach out, grab her and kiss her until she forgave him, but common sense warned him to stay where he was.

"How long was I gone before you two started hooking up?" Asa glared, hurt and betrayed.

"It wasn't like that," he clarified. "About a month ago, Brian and I went to a party. She was there. We were all drinking and having fun. The next thing I remember was waking up in my SUV with Misty beside me. Everything else is just a blur."

"I guess congratulations are in order," she spoke matter-of-factly.

"Don't be angry," he begged, wishing he could rewind the last few moments.

"How can I not be? I lo—" Her words suddenly stopped, and her expression went completely blank.

The lively woman standing in front of him disappeared and was replaced by the sullen girl he first met all those years ago. Silently, she leered at him, dark eyes even darker with rage. Before he could stop her, she climbed down the ladder and ran inside the house, slamming the door behind her, leaving him sitting alone on the roof, wishing he could get sucked up into a passing UFO.

The morning had started horribly when Asa woke with a screaming headache that transformed into a mind-numbing migraine. Then she went to take a shower, and the water heater had gone on the fritz. That was quickly followed by her being extra clumsy and spilling an entire carton of creamer onto the kitchen counter and floor. It couldn't possibly get any worse.

Regardless of her early morning setbacks, Asa managed to make her way to the Cherry Creek Shopping Center, locate the upscale boutique where Misty worked, and successfully snuck in undetected while the blonde troglodyte rang up several customers. Stealthily, she hid, waiting for the right time to confront the woman who was bound and determined to ruin her future with Ian Granger.

"Hope you have a great time at the party," Misty called to the leaving customer.

Asa waited several minutes before stepping out from behind a tall dress rack and was about to confront the other woman when a burly blonde man wearing a blue flannel shirt and worn jeans came in. Immediately, she stilled, waiting for the man to make his purchase and leave.

"What the hell are you doing here?" Misty snarled, motioning him to move away from the glass doors. "I told you I don't want to talk with you."

"How was your doctor's appointment?" the unfamiliar man's posture stiffened.

"Good," she spoke with a hushed tone. "The next time, I'll get a sonogram of the baby."

"You're definitely pregnant?" he asked bleakly.

"I've told you already, I took a home pregnancy test, and it came out positive," the frustrated female sighed. "The doctor's visit just confirmed it. Don't look so worried. I'm not even sure the baby is yours."

"But we had sex," he bristled.

"I know, but you know there was someone else," Misty answered meekly, unable to make direct eye contact with the aggravated male.

Nervously, Misty began organizing her counter area and then quickly moved on to putting clothes on hangers and retagging them with clearance stickers. When the silence was too deafening for both parties, the man spoke.

"Does this other guy love you?" he grilled, scrubbing an irritated hand over his facial stubbles.

"No," she replied firmly.

"I'm not playing this game with you, Misty," the guy bristled. "You know how I feel about the pregnancy. It's still early. You can—"

"I'm not terminating the pregnancy," Misty cringed.

"Do what you want," the man growled. "But don't expect me to—"

"I don't expect anything from you, Tommy," Misty growled back, eyes narrowed, lips set in a thin line.

Asa suddenly felt a little sorry for her.

A little.

"Tommy, please leave before my boss gets back and hears us arguing," her rival begged. "I can't afford to lose this job."

"See ya," Tommy grumbled as he turned and left the store.

When the coast was finally clear, Asa stepped out from behind the tall rack of clothing.

"How much is this?" she queried, a smile playing at her lips, but it didn't reach her eyes.

Misty's frustration was immediately replaced with a nervous frown.

"Asa, you're back," Misty mumbled.

"How perceptive of you to notice," She touched the delicate fabric of one of the dresses with an approving stroke. "I've heard you've been busy."

"Busy?" the lady smiled uneasily.

"Yeah, you know, working here, attending parties, *getting pregnant*," Asa commented, observing the other woman's skittish demeanor.

"Ian told you," Misty swallowed hard.

"He did," she responded, moving to a rack of multicolored halter tops.

A sage green one with delicate strands of gold thread caught her eye, and she stopped momentarily to check the price tag. Fifty-five dollars? For a scrap of fabric? It was too rich for her blood.

"After hearing your conversation, I didn't mean to eavesdrop," she informed. "But the two of you were arguing so loudly I couldn't help overhearing. I've put two and two together, by the way."

Misty's face paled as Asa's words sunk in.

"I was going to tell Ian, but I wanted to wait until after the baby was born to get the paternity test," Misty admitted sincerely, and Asa believed her.

"You slept with two men on the same night and don't know whom the baby belongs to. Is that the gist of it?"

Misty's eyes welled, and Asa began to really feel sorry for her.

"Listen, I feel sorry for you, but if the baby is Ian's, you know he'll do the honorable thing."

"You mean marry me?" Misty's hushed words made Asa's heart clench, but she covered it up as best as she could.

Unexpectedly, Asa felt the room begin to spin, and try as she might, she couldn't stay on her feet. Thank goodness a chair was close by and easy to access. Her entire world was crashing down around her, and all she could do was sit and cringe at the thought of Ian marrying someone else.

"Possibly," was the only word Asa could manage.

"I know he doesn't love me," her foe whispered. "His heart has always belonged to you."

That fact didn't make Asa feel any less hurt.

"Good luck, Misty," Asa gave a small smile. "I'm sure everything will be as it should."

"Thanks, Asa," Misty replied.

Asa turned to leave, but her childhood bully halted her.

"Do you know the reason why I always teased you and called you names growing up?"

Asa shook her head.

"I was jealous of you."

"Jealous of me?" Asa scoffed. "Why?"

"You've never cared what other people thought of you," Misty complimented. "You did what you wanted when you wanted. Your best friend is a guy, for Pete's sake."

"I guess that is kind of strange," she admitted with a small grin.

"And you don't take shit from anyone," Misty continued.

"Ian says I'm too stubborn," Asa chuckled.

"I've always had a crush on Ian," Misty added somberly.

"I know," she stiffened.

"The only reason he slept with me was because he was drunk and missing you, and I took advantage of his condition," her rival clarified.

"You seduced him, not the other way around?" Asa acknowledged without heat.

Misty nodded.

"He talked about you the entire summer, wouldn't shut up, actually. Asa's in Brazil. Asa sent me pictures from the Serengeti. Asa photographed Great White Sharks at the Great Barrier Reef," the other woman sighed. "He's so proud of you."

"I didn't realize," she mumbled, surprised at the news.

"And the way he looks at you when you don't know he's watching you… I would give anything for a man to look at me just once with as much longing and admiration as Ian looks at you."

Finally, Asa sighed, realization battering her anger until it began to seep away.

"You've got an amazing man, and you continuously push him away," Misty warned. "Be careful. One day you might push too hard and lose him altogether."

Asa nodded before leaving the boutique.

What a colossal clusterfuck!

The Granger house smelled wonderful: spicy, fragrant, and mouthwatering. Whatever Ian was cooking made her stomach grumble, and her mouth salivate. He was definitely meant to be a chef.

"What are you doing here?" Ian snapped as he took out his chopping board and chef's knife.

"I saw your parents leaving," Asa admitted. "Your mom told me you were working on a few new recipes."

"I didn't think I'd ever see you again," Ian paused, staring at her, blue eyes lined red from a lack of sleep. "It's been over a month since our last conversation."

"Has it been that long?"

Unamused, he glared at her angrily.

"I'm sorry," she sincerely apologized, walking around the breakfast bar to stand beside him. "I was hurt and shocked and—"

"I know," he whispered, resting the knife on the counter and turning to face her, and the desperation in his eyes lanced her heart. "What am I going to do if it is my baby?"

"We are going to love it," she stated with a weak smile.

"We?"

"Yes… *we*," Asa told firmly, her eyes welling. "If it is yours, then *we* will love it and arrange visits and sleepovers and help Misty raise it."

"You're amazing." Ian grabbed her and hugged her tightly, burying his face at the side of her neck and enjoying her warmth.

"I know," she giggled. "Just remember that."

Chapter Ten

Seven and a half months later…

"He's gorgeous," Asa whispered as she held the tiny bundle swaddled in the generic blue, white, and green striped hospital blanket in her arms. "What's his name?"

"I haven't decided yet," Misty frowned. Her face glowed, but her eyes looked exhausted.

Ian stood beside Asa, looking at the little round face looking back up at him.

"I think he has my eyes." Ian gave the baby his finger to hold. "He looks healthy."

"The doctor says he's perfect… ten fingers… ten toes…" the new mom yawned sleepily.

"Why don't you take a nap?" Asa suggested, acknowledging the fact that she needed some rest after almost twelve hours of labor. "We can stay for a while."

"Thanks." Misty yawned again as she closed her eyes. "I think an hour's nap should do the trick."

Ian held his arms out, and Asa gently placed the now sleeping baby into them. "When are they going to take the cultures for the paternity test?" she asked, stroking the baby's soft skin with tender touches.

Ian sat in the nearby chair before looking up at her.

"They've already swabbed my cheek and his and sent the samples to the lab. I asked to put a rush on it. We should know by tomorrow."

"That's fast," Asa mumbled nervously, perching on the arm of the chair where he currently sat.

"I've gotten used to the idea that he might be mine," Ian admitted, placing a lingering kiss to the baby's forehead; the bundle stirred but didn't wake.

Asa bent, giving Ian a chaste kiss on the lips.

"Have you decided what you're gonna do if he is?"

He shook his head but wouldn't make eye contact with her. A gloomy sigh rushed past her lips, and her hands began to tremble. She already knew the answer. Ian was an honorable man. He'd do the right thing.

A soft knock on her door made her look up from her *Andy Rouse* wildlife photography book.

"Come in," she responded, not able to hide the desperation she felt.

"Dinner is ready," her mom said, a similar expression on her face. "Why don't you come downstairs and eat with us?"

"I'm not hungry," Asa turned back to her book.

"You haven't eaten much these last few days."

"I'm too upset to eat," Asa pouted, feeling the acid in her stomach sloshing around.

"You're going to make yourself sick—"

"Mom," she huffed, taking off her reading glasses and almost throwing them down on the bed beside her. "I said I'm not hungry. I'm a grown woman. If I'm hungry, I'll eat."

Her mother tensed but turned and left without argument. Asa had hardly left her room since the day at the hospital when Ian's paternity test results came back one hundred percent certain that he was the biological father. She hadn't been able to stop crying since.

Ian had called her several times, but she had let them go to voicemail. And in one last attempt to avoid the dreaded conversation that was quickly approaching, she locked herself in her bedroom and refused to leave except to go to the gallery or to her college classes.

Another knock made her look up, but when she went to the door to yell at whoever was bothering her, there was no one there. The knocking started again, but this time she looked toward the window.

Ian.

Ignoring him, she went to lie on the bed.

"Open the window," he ordered, face flushed and grim.

If he wasn't so handsome, she would have left him on the ladder outside of her window.

"I don't want to talk to you," she responded and continued to read.

"I thought we were going to do this together," her best friend reminded. "Isn't that what you said?"

"That was before you decided to marry her," Asa blurted in a hushed tone, tears freely falling now and landing on the pages of her book.

"What did you say?"

Silence.

"You've got it all wrong, Asa."

"Really?" Asa gasped, wiping her tears with the back of her hands. "I don't think I do. I understand that you're trying to do the right thing, but… but…."

She was sobbing now, and the pathetic act caused her even more distress.

"Ian, go home."

"Not until you hear me out," he demanded gruffly.

"Tell me where you two are registered," she sniffled, "I'll buy you a wedding present."

"Stop being so… *you*… and open the damn window before I fall and break my neck!"

Rolling her eyes, she sat contemplating his words. After a few tense moments, she opened it and let him in.

"I don't know why I put up with you sometimes," he snarled and shook his head.

"Me?!" she questioned harshly. "I'm not the one who attracts trouble."

She was pacing now, looking frazzled but delicious at the same time.

"Could you please sit and listen to what I have to say?" Ian pleaded.

"Give me one good reason why I should!" Asa bellowed, not caring who heard.

"I'll give you two reasons: because I love you and because I want to marry you!" he matched her volume.

"Is this some kind of joke?" she hissed. "If it is, it's not funny. It is cruel."

She swiped at the tears that continued to escape.

"How can we get married?" Asa sobbed. "What about Misty?"

"If you had picked up the damned phone when I called you, you could have saved yourself from all of this unnecessary drama," Ian reprimanded, shaking his head in frustration.

That statement earned him a swift kick to the shin.

"Ouch!" he yelled, followed by a string of profanity that would have made a veteran sailor blush. "What the hell was that for?"

"That was for being an asshole, that's what!" she accused with a huff, feeling a little better since he was in pain too. "Hurry up and tell me whatever it is that you wanted to tell me."

"A few days ago, Misty dropped off the baby and said she had a few errands to run. I didn't think anything of it, but when a few hours turned into overnight, I started to get worried."

"What?" Asa gasped loudly.

"Shh!" he chastised. "I'm still explaining."

Asa's mouth slammed close, but she gave him a patented *you-are-a-complete-jock-stain* stare.

"When she didn't come back for the baby, I called her cell. To my surprise, the number was no longer in service."

Asa's heartbeat quickened as she got pulled into his story.

"In a state of panic, I called her folks. They hadn't seen her in over twenty-four hours," Ian rambled. "Finally, I got desperate and went to the boutique where she worked and spoke to the owner. She told me Misty quit last week. She told her boss she was going away with some guy name Tommy... something-or-another. I can't remember his last name."

"She abandoned her baby?" Asa's mouth went dry.

"I think so," he grimaced. "Fuckin' shit!"

"Did you contact the police?"

He nodded.

"What did they say?"

"I had to file a report and contact DCF. They've got to do some investigating, but they said I would be able to get full custody if she really did abandon him."

"Holy crap!" she mumbled under her breath. "Holy! Crap!"

Suddenly, he grabbed her around the waist roughly and pulled her against his hard-as-granite chest. The scent of body wash and his unique essence made her swoon. She didn't even try to hide how his nearness affected her.

"And you, woman," he growled. "Made a bad situation worse."

"What do you mean?" she sneered, trying to pull away, but he held her securely.

"I was never going to marry Misty," Ian explained through gritted teeth. "I was going to file for joint custody and marry you—you damn stubborn female."

"I don't want to marry you," Asa blatantly lied, glaring at him with the hope he would spontaneously combust.

"Yes, you do," he smirked.

"Says who?" she mocked.

An arched brow was his only response, and as if she weighed nothing at all, he threw her over his shoulder in a fireman's hold.

"Put me down, Ian!" she squealed. "What the hell do you think you're doing?"

"I'm giving you something that you've deserved since the first day I met you on the roof of this house."

"What are you talking about?" She squirmed, trying to break free of his steely hold.

"Do you know what you put me through this week? I've been dealing with the whole Misty situation, which was bad enough as it is, but then throw in the fact that you had completely shut me off and refused to answer my calls," his voice rose and transformed into a menacing sound that scared her a bit. "For all I knew, you had packed up your duffle bag and had left the country *again*."

She held her tongue, refusing to reveal she had thought of doing just that.

Sitting down at the edge of the bed, he arranged her on his lap, ass up, and roughly pulled up her gauze skirt and pulled down her white lace panties, throwing the strip of fabric onto the carpet. She gasped loudly and fought his hold, but in the end, he was much too strong for her to escape his determined grip.

"Damn it, Ian. Let me go!" she whined. "I'm a grown woman!"

Her mouth gaped at the realization he was going to spank her.

"Ian, stop it this instant!"

"Nope," he chuckled, enjoying her panic. "You deserve this."

"I'm not the one who screwed a tramp!" she verbally assaulted. "You did this yourself!"

"On that point, you're absolutely right, but you should have known that I don't want to spend my life with anyone else except you. you… stubborn… violent… brooding… relentless—"

He rubbed her naked bottom with the palm of his hand right before he spanked her, not too hard, but hard enough to make his point. The sound as his palm made contact with her bare backside was far worse than the impact itself.

Actually, she liked it.

"Stop!" she yelled, hoping her parents would hear and come to her rescue.

Damn it! Her parents might hear.

"Ian," her voice lowered. "My parents are downstairs."

"I know," he grinned, not caring who heard and not telling her that her parents had seen him climbing up the ladder to her room when they were leaving for the specialty food market in the city and wouldn't be back for a few hours. "They are gonna hear you getting the spanking you deserve, and you know what they're going to do?"

He smacked her now pink ass harder before announcing loudly, "Absolutely nothing."

Three more erotic slaps landed before he yanked her to a sitting position and kissed her passionately.

"I love you, Asa, and that's never gonna change. No matter how much you wanna push me away, I'm still gonna be here. And I know that I fucked up royally with this whole Misty business, but you're the only one I've ever loved. Do you understand me?"

She nodded right before she reclaimed his lips, and when she finally pulled away, they were both breathless.

"Nineteen is kinda young to get married, don't you think?" She winced, trying to ignore her slightly aching butt.

"We'll both be twenty in a few months," he reminded, moving her long hair out of the way, so he could kiss her neck.

"What about your degree?"

"I'll postpone it," he announced, lavishing her neck with licks and nips he knew would make her just as needy as him.

"You can't do that." Asa angled her head to give him better access. "We'll all move to Hyde Park while you finish your Bachelor's Degree. I'll see if my boss at the gallery can use her connections to get me a job at a museum there, and I'll take a few online classes as well."

"What about the baby?" Ian questioned, his mind focused on getting inside of her.

"We'll figure it out. Lots of parents deal with it; we can too," she gasped when his hand slipped under her blouse and found her hardened nipple, rolling the bud with mischievous fingers.

"I've missed this," he said with gleeful admiration.

She moaned when he gave the peak a pinch.

"Where are we going to live?"

"We'll get an apartment or rent a house near the college that has reasonable student rates," he stated with a smile. "I'll get a part-time job to make ends meet. I've got a full scholarship for school. At least that's taken care of."

"You make it sound easy," she moaned again, unable to contain the sound.

Desperately, he nuzzled her collarbone with his nose.

"I know I'm asking a lot of you," Ian huffed. "Giving up your independence to marry a guy with a newborn baby, no money, no nothing—"

"I haven't agreed to marry you," she looked at him warily.

"I assumed—"

"You haven't asked me yet, idiot," Asa teased, elbowing him in the ribcage, making him wince.

"I guess I'm getting ahead of myself," he chuckled low as he kissed a line heading south to more exotic locations.

Asa moaned when he landed on her left nipple; the excited peak was even harder and awaiting his attention. With a boldness she'd never felt from him before, he sucked the entire nipple, shirt and all, into his hot wet mouth. The strong pulling sensation made her panties dampen and her clit pulse with want.

"We can't do this now," she informed, pushing him away, but he held her tighter. "My parents will definitely hear us."

Her face heated at the thought of them interrupting their romp.

"Who's watching the baby?" she tried distracting him.

"Mom and Dad," he educated, grabbing the front of her blouse and pulling the two halves of the material apart. The sound of popping buttons made him smile and her frown.

"This *was* my favorite shirt," she snarled with a wicked smile.

"I'll buy you another one," he scoffed, pulling down the cups of her bra to get a better view of her heaving breasts, and then he joked, "When we get married, you're not allowed to wear underwear ever again."

"You wish," she said, rolling her eyes and staring at the door, hoping no one was on the other side listening. He tweaked her nipple, making her yelp, then soothed the sting with the tip of his tongue. The dual sensation made another trickle of arousal seep from her core. "Brute."

Ian laughed, suckled the perky mound, then released it and repeated the process with its twin.

"I'm so turned on. I know this is going to be a quick fuck," he announced. "Then I'm going to make love to you. Nice and slow until you come."

"What about my parents?" she reminded once more.

"Didn't I tell you they left for town about twenty minutes ago?" he chuckled.

Feeling foolish, Asa playfully bit his shoulder in retaliation which made him shout.

"Do you want another spanking?"

One of Ian's dark brows hitched when she smiled and nodded in response. Utterly flabbergasted, he laughed until he almost cried.

Asa, his exotic wildcat… always surprised him.

"Next time," he emphatically reassured.

Acting on instinct, Ian moved his hand lower and slipped one thick digit into her soaked channel.

"You're dripping," he conveyed in awe. "Did the spanking turn you on?"

Embarrassed beyond belief, Asa blushed.

"Damn, I love you!" he exclaimed, pulling her closer and ravaging her mouth with desperate kisses.

Picking her up again, he moved her to the middle of the bed.

"This is gonna be hard and fast. I've been dreaming about fucking this tight pussy all week. I don't think I'm gonna last very long."

She nodded.

"I promise I'll make it up to you."

"You better," she said, giving him a haughty snort. "You need a condom."

Then he stilled.

"Shit! I don't have any with me."

"That's okay," the love of his life smirked. "I picked up a box, just in case."

With that, she reached into the top drawer of the nightstand, pulled out a foil wrapper, and handed it to him.

"Wait."

Suddenly, he stood, ripped his t-shirt over his head, and threw it on the floor, then made quick work of the rest of his unneeded and unwanted clothing. Climbing on the bed, he arranged her legs until they were spread eagle as wide as he could get them.

"Put it on me," he ordered, his face pained, eyes glistening.

"I've never—"

"It's easy. Place it at the tip and roll it down. Be careful," he blushed. "We wouldn't want it to break."

Asa snorted at his ironic remark and rolled her eyes. She quickly sheathed his cock in a few rolls, smiling at her work.

Without preamble, he knelt between her legs, grabbed his cock, and breached her to the hilt in one determined lunge. She gasped as the entire rock-hard length registered in her sex as well as her brain.

My goodness! She thought the man was hung like an elephant.

The slight pain made her wild and hitched up her arousal another notch.

"I'm never gonna get enough of you, my little wildcat," he remarked, gorging on her nipple as he began plunging inside of her wildly. Arching her back, she met him thrust for thrust, moaning and cursing the entire time. The breathy sounds only added to his untimely release.

"*Fuck!*" he growled, and his entire body tensed as he filled the condom. His shaking arms buckled, and he landed on Asa's half-exposed breasts.

"That *was* quick," Asa glared at him.

"I know you haven't come yet. I'll fix that," he promised, pulling out of her and discarding the used condom in the trashcan beside the nightstand.

Moving lower, he buried his face in her vagina, using his tongue to totally devastate her soaked sex. Enthusiastically, he speared the talented muscle and fucked her like it was a miniature version of the real thing, which was now stiff and ready, willing, and able for round two.

"Holy shit, that feels wonderful," she purred, grabbing a fistful of his hair and securing his face in position. "I don't even want to know how you got so good at doing this."

"You are so wet," he whispered and went for her clit next, lapping up her sweet cream and needing her to come before he entered her for the second time. Asa's body stiffened as her inner muscles clenched but found nothing to latch onto.

"I need—"

He understood the request and complied by breaching her with two thick fingers, pumping steadily to the movements of her hips.

"Come for me," he ordered, increasing the speed of his thrusts as he leaned down and sucked her clit until she screamed her release.

"Pass me another condom."

Ian quickly suited up. Before she came down from her orgasm, he flipped her over.

"Get on your hands and knees," his voice sounded harsh. Instantly, she followed his command.

When she was in place, he entered her still pulsating channel and slowly worked his cock inside of her, enjoying every hitch of her breath, every shudder of her petite frame, and every soft moan that rushed past her parted lips. Unhurried, he fucked her until his eyes rolled back in his head as Asa came again. Her tightening muscles massaged his cock with invisible fingers as he spilled every last bit of seed inside the second condom.

"Marry me," his words rushed out in a choppy jumble. Holding his breath, he impatiently awaited her answer.

"I guess so," she teased after an excruciating length of time. "Someone has to save that poor baby from being raised by you."

Leaning forward, he kissed her on the shoulder blade.

"I love you, Asa."

"I love you, too, Ian."

Chapter Eleven

They got married on the Fourth of July in a small yet elegant ceremony. Asa wore her mom's vintage wedding gown and looked spectacular. Her hair in an updo, classic pearl earrings, and a matching necklace completed the look. Ian wore a classic black suit sans neckwear and looked equally as dashing if he said so himself. Even their adorable two-month-old son, Adam, was dressed in a little suit.

Surprisingly, everything came together seamlessly except for their rings. Unfortunately, they couldn't afford expensive wedding bands, so they bought inexpensive gold bands at a local chain department store. Asa reassured him that she didn't care about a pricey bridal set, but he knew otherwise. He loved her even more for saying it. He'd be sure to buy her an incredible ring in the near future.

The traditional wedding ceremony, performed by the local non-denominational minister who lived about a mile away, was heartfelt yet simple. Each wrote their own vows and was surprised that they made most of their guests cry, especially both sets of parents. Adam was the only one who didn't shed a tear.

Fortunately, the reception was just as beautiful. The festivities were also held in the backyard inside a specialty tent that was decorated to resemble a grand ballroom of a fancy hotel. Asa had seen something similar in Steve Martin's movie *Father of the Bride*.

The impressive space was adorned with two elegant silver chandeliers hung from the high ceiling that illuminated the parquet dance floor below. Six round tables ornamented with bright white tablecloths, full china, and silverware wrapped in white linen napkins lay perfectly beside each place setting while tall glass vases in various shapes filled with striking white calla lilies graced the middle of each table. The space glowed like something out of a dream, and the four-piece string ensemble they had hired for the evening filled the sublime space with music that seemed to come from the angels themselves.

"My mom is ready to serve dinner." Asa appeared and hugged him from behind. The soothing rose fragrance surrounding her made him smile.

"Great, I'm starving," he mentioned for the tenth time, kissing the tip of the nose.

In order to keep the cost manageable, he and Mrs. Addams—his new mother-in-law—created the menu and prepped and prepared the food. Making it a buffet made it easy for everyone to serve themselves. They would clean up tomorrow.

Sitting at the newlywed table off to the side, Ian and his new bride chatted as they feasted on an appetizer of pan-seared scallops with spicy chorizo, followed by a mouthwatering entre of Steak Diane, succulent grilled Atlantic prawns, Parisian-style new potatoes, and a medley of baby vegetables. Both he and Asa ate with gusto.

"You and Mom did a fantastic job with the food," Asa purred, the sound instantly making his dick hard.

"Wait til you see the cake," Ian added, switching the theme of the conversation to the secret matrimonial concoction.

"I can't believe you haven't let me see it yet," she chastised without heat. "Even after I performed that blow-job you requested."

Her playful pout made him laugh.

"I wanted it to be a surprise," he said, kissing her cheek and wishing they could leave early for the honeymoon.

As they spoke, the quartet returned from their fifteen-minute break, and immediately Asa's favorite instrumental composition of *Counting Stars* began to play. Removing the napkin from his lap, he stood and held out his hand to her.

"Mrs. Granger, would you do me the honor of dancing with me."

She sat for a second, sizing him up.

"I'm not sure," his new bride teased with a mischievous glint in her sparkling irises. "The last time we slow danced, you stepped on my toes so many times I thought you were stomping grapes."

"I've been practicing with my mom," Ian bashfully admitted. "I promise there will be no winemaking."

"Please, be careful," Asa begged with a nervous grin. "I'm wearing open-toed shoes, and it'll really hurt."

"Come on." He pulled her to a standing position and led her to the middle of the dance floor.

To her amazement, her handsome groom waltzed her around the space with practiced refinement.

"Wow! I'll have to nickname you Fred Astaire."

After the song was finished, the cake was wheeled out. Anxiously, he watched her reaction as the three-tiered confection came into view. Just as he had hoped, her gasp almost sucked all of the air out of the space, and quite unexpectedly, her dark eyes welled with tears, and she dabbed at the corners to keep her make-up from smudging.

"Say something," he requested when she stood stock-still, eyes glistening under the soft glow of the overhead lighting.

It was perfect. The intricately decorated all-white cake took her breath away. Sugared calla lilies adorned the top tier, while the second and third layers were simply decorated with hand-piped pearls like the ones in the jewelry she wore. It was everything she had hoped for and more.

"Let's just say you'll be getting more than just a blowjob tonight, Mr. Granger," she winked and squeezed his firm ass.

"I'm holding you to that, Mrs. Granger," he winked back.

Chapter Twelve

Six months later…

"Where are my knives?" Ian groaned as he ran around their scantily decorated two-bedroom / two-bath, single-story ranch house in Poughkeepsie, New York less than ten minutes from the famed *Culinary Institute of America* in Hyde Park.

"Lower your voice," Asa whispered, closing the door to Adam's room. "I just got him to sleep, and I don't want you waking him."

"Sorry," her husband's voice instantly hushed.

"Where was the last place you had them?"

"If I knew that I wouldn't be hunting for them, would I?" he answered rather haughtily.

"Don't be sarcastic with me, Ian David Granger," she warned. The tone of her voice and the use of his full name made him pause.

"I'm sorry," he apologized sincerely, kissing her chastely on the cheek. "I don't want to be late for class. My instructor is a real stickler for the rules."

Understanding dawned, and her posture softened.

"Did you use them last night while practicing your filleting technique?"

"Yes," he grinned, running past her into the galley kitchen. "Found them!"

He chuckled as he reappeared carrying the wooden cutlery box out of the pantry.

"What were they doing in there?" she inquired, giggling at her husband's absentmindedness.

"I got distracted when Adam started crying last night," Ian admitted. "I must have thrown them in there."

"I see," she grinned, picking up their son's toys from the play mat. "You'd lose your head if it wasn't attached."

"What's your schedule like today?" he questioned only half listening.

"I've got to work on my photography portfolio that's due at the end of the semester. Adam has an appointment at the pediatrician's office in the afternoon and I've got to go to work this evening for a few hours to help set up for the new art exhibit at the gallery tomorrow night."

Overwhelmed, Asa threw herself down on the sofa and covered her eyes.

"And I still need to go grocery shopping, pay the electric bill before they turn it off, and—"

"Ok, stop," he lovingly urged, sitting beside her and hugging her gently. "I'll pick up the groceries on my way home and if you give me the electric bill, I can do that too."

"That would really help, thank you," she sighed, then rested her head on his shoulder.

"I don't know how you do it," he said, kissing her sweetly.

"Me either." Asa gazed at him, a fatigued mask covering her beautiful features. "Are you working at the restaurant this weekend?"

"Yeah," he responded, releasing her and gathering up the rest of his school supplies. "The sous chef is going out of town for the weekend, and the head chef asked me to fill in for her."

"That's awesome," she stated proudly. "He must be impressed with your skills."

"I think so," Ian replied happily.

Glancing at the clock, he kissed her again, got the utility bill and shopping list, grabbed his backpack, and ran toward the front door.

"I'll call you on my break."

Asa nodded and settled on the sofa for a short nap before Adam woke from his. For the life of her, she didn't understand how her parents did this and made it look so easy. She would never roll her eyes at them again.

It was almost night, and there were not enough hours in the day to get everything done. Laundry was piling up, and so were the dirty dishes. They were down to the last roll of toilet paper, Adam had been cranky for the entire afternoon, and she couldn't figure out why.

Counting Stars

Asa breathed a sigh of relief when she heard Ian's vehicle pull into the driveway, and soon after, his footsteps echoed on the concrete as he walked toward the house.

"You're late," Asa scolded, handing the baby to Ian as he walked through the front door. "I've got to be at the gallery in fifteen minutes!"

"I got stuck behind a lady with over a hundred coupons and had to wait since there was only one cashier on duty," he informed in good spirits. "Good news is, the lady gave me several coupons that saved us over six bucks on diapers, formula, paper towels, and cereal."

"That's great, but you can tell me all about it tonight," his wife blurted in a frenzy.

After kissing his cheek, she grabbed her purse and left him holding Adam, who was cooing, laughing, and having a wonderful time watching her husband making funny faces.

"See you guys later."

"See ya, Mommy," her husband replied in a baby-sized voice that made her smile.

She loved her two men.

Both were adorable.

Both were irresistible.

And both were making her late for work.

Three and half hours later, Asa returned home to a romantic setting of lighted candles, a red and white checkered tablecloth spread out picnic-style on the living room floor, and the aroma of something delicious cooking. She smiled to herself as she locked the deadbolt behind her. Happily, she glanced around the open area for her thoughtful husband.

"Ian?" she called softly, unsure if the baby was asleep. "Where are you?"

"I'm out back," his deep voice wafted through the opened glass door.

Thrilled to be back home, Asa rested her keys and purse on the countertop; she followed his seductive timbre outside to the back deck, where she found him grilling chicken and various vegetables on their hibachi grill.

"Dinner smells amazing," she complimented, bending low to deliver a much-deserved kiss to his full mouth. "Is it almost ready?"

"Uh-huh," he acknowledged, turning the skewers of mushrooms, bell peppers, onions, and zucchini and basting them with garlic and rosemary-infused olive oil. "How was work?"

"Busy but fun," she grinned, sitting on one of their plastic patio chairs. "The visiting Picasso exhibit is ready for tomorrow's grand reveal."

Slowly, her eyes roamed over his profile, admiring his classic bone structure. *She'd never grow tired of looking at him.*

"How was your day?"

"I got on an A on my sauces practicum." A boyish grin covered his face; the goofy expression made him look much younger than his twenty years. "I think my instructor was pleased."

"How can you see what you're doing?" Asa grumbled as she looked around the dark space, fumbling for the light switch. "I'll turn on the light—"

"Wait!" he protested, but his word escaped too late. His body stiffened when she realized…

"You forgot to pay the electric bill?"

The disappointment in her voice made him feel like a complete ass. Without argument, she stood and went back inside the house, flipping the light switches she walked past.

"Great!"

Following at a safe distance, he agreed.

"I know I screwed up, but in my defense, I did remember to do the shopping, and I've made a delicious dinner."

Asa shot him a cold stare.

"I've already called and paid the bill," Ian explained. "They'll have it turned back on before eleven tonight."

"It's seven o'clock now," she huffed, throwing herself face down on the sofa wishing she had gotten a longer nap. "What are we going to do for four hours in the dark?"

Honestly, he could think of at least twenty things he'd like to do to his sulking wife that didn't require electricity or clothing, but in her current mood, he decided to keep that list to himself.

"Go change outta your work clothes, and when you come back, we can eat," he stated, helping her to her feet.

She nodded and did as he asked. While she was gone, he plated their meals, poured them a couple of glasses of juice, and waited patiently at his romantic indoor picnic. A few minutes later, she returned looking just as forlorn as when she left. Hopefully, a hot meal would raise her spirits.

Surprisingly, he was right. Asa finished her dinner and asked for seconds, which she seldom did.

"This is delicious," she purred, cleaning her plate for the second time. "I love that I'm married to a chef."

He eyed her warily before asking, "Am I forgiven?"

"Possibly," she teased, tapping her pouty bottom lip with her index finger.

The deliberate motion called attention to her more than kissable mouth. Cautiously, he leaned forward, waiting for her to do the same. When she stood instead, he felt his heart skip a beat.

Damn! She was still upset.

Standing over him with a heated gaze, she began unbuttoning her blouse. *WTF!* He *was* forgiven! After the last button was undone, she let the garment fall from her shoulders onto the floor behind her. He had to run his hand across his mouth to make sure there was no drool.

Next were the jeans. His palms began to sweat as Asa unbuttoned and unzipped in front of his wandering eyes. His wife was stunning. Flawless cream complexion, hypnotic almond-shaped onyx eyes, plump lips that begged to be sampled, and a body most women would pay thousands of dollars to possess.

As he continued to watch, she reached behind her back and unhooked her bra, letting it fall from her in a casual motion. His breath hitched at the sight of her almost naked. Finally, she hooked her thumbs into the waistband of her silky black panties and slowly wiggled them down her shapely legs.

"You've been a bad boy," she condemned, voice low and raspy; the sound floated past her lips and caressed his cock until it strained against the fly of his jeans.

"Yes," he agreed. "I have been an *extremely* naughty boy."

"Come here," she commanded, crooking a finger at him. When he was almost within arm's length, she turned to leave, giving him a perfect view of her round, firm ass.

Oh yeah! He was a lucky man.

"Whatever you want," he swallowed hard, wanting to reach out and touch her but refraining. As they made their way into the bathroom, she closed the door, sealing them inside. Finding the lighter, she lighted the scented candle sitting on the top shelf of the space-saver cabinet.

"Take off your clothes," she requested in that wicked voice. Obediently, he wasted no time as he stripped off his clothes and dropped them absently onto the tiled floor. "Kneel."

Huh?

He made the mistake of hesitating, which earned him a no-nonsense glare. Playing along, he knelt in front of her. The second blunder of reaching out to touch her bare legs was rewarded with another irate look.

"Tsk, tsk, tsk," she warned, lips curling into a mischievous semi-smile.

"I can't touch you. Is that what you're telling me?" he asked, trying to figure out the game.

"You are correct, Slave," she replied with a straight face.

"Asa—"

"No… it's *Mistress* to you." Her rough words, accompanied by an arrogant smirk, caused his cock to grow another painful inch.

"You're joking, right?" Impudently, she shook her head, and he was forced to amend, saying, "I'm supposed to let you boss me around and call me a slave?"

"Only if you want sex tonight." She turned, giving him another tempting view of her naked backside.

Ian didn't have to think very long before saying, "What would you like me to do," he paused, swallowed what little moisture was left in his mouth, "Mistress?"

Asa smiled.

"Turn on the shower and adjust the temperature."

Without hesitation, he followed her command, helped her inside the enclosure, and then waited for her next order.

"Wash me," she said, handing him the natural sea sponge and the bottle of body wash. "Your hands are not to touch me; is that clear?"

He didn't know if he liked this game anymore.

"Yes, Mistress."

Chuckling, she stepped into the heated spray of the showerhead. They were both relieved the water heater still contained hot water. If his wife had to take a frigid shower, she'd never have sex with him again.

Ian washed her thoroughly, a little too thoroughly for her liking. Efficiently, he started from her neck, down her shoulders, under her arms, over her torso and abdomen, and finally kneeling in front of her to lather her legs and feet.

"What about the other parts?" Asa wondered why he had avoided her vagina and bottom.

"Mistress didn't specify the areas her slave is supposed to wash." With a devilish grin, he stared. "I didn't want to be flogged."

"Is that right?" his wife snickered.

"Uh-huh," he smirked, but her feral grin caused him to reexamine his previous statement.

"Tell me what you want me to do." Instantly, his mind went to several outlandish ideas.

"Nothing," she beamed, watching him, watching her.

Surprise sideswiped his brain, and one brow hitched with confusion as he blurted, "Pardon me?"

"I wouldn't want my slave to become too overworked or overheated." Asa smiled.

He didn't see that one coming.

"I'll take care of it myself. You can just *watch*."

At her sultry declaration, Ian swallowed the large lump that had suddenly formed in his throat, and as he continued to stare, his wife took her slender hand and ran it along her skin until it was cupping one heavy mound, eager fingers pinched a dark nipple.

Now he understood. She was going to pleasure herself.

Fuck a duck!

A soft whimper escaped her parted lips as she slipped a hand between her supple thighs. With teasing slowness, she found the entrance to her sex and immediately plunged two fingers inside. Using the heel of her hand, she massaged her aching clit. Ian's breathing accelerated at the erotic sight of his sexy woman pleasuring herself.

"I want to kiss you there," he said, nodding in the direction of her slowly pumping fingers. The painful ache in his balls reminded him of his own needs.

"Not yet," she panted, continuing the all too distracting movement.

Ian groaned as he took his hard length in his eager hand and began stroking it in time with her plunges.

"Ok," he begged. "I've been punished long enough."

There was no response.

Pushing her fingers deeper, she began to pump in time to an unheard beat, pressing the heel of her hand against the aching bud a little harder. A breathy moan came from her as she widened her toned legs and leaned against the cool tiles of the shower wall. Satisfaction surrounded her as her husband's heated gaze swept over her.

In a calculated mental assault, Asa reached up and detached the showerhead, quickly setting it to a harder flow and directing the pulsating stream at her clit. Ian's eyes grew to unimaginable proportions; her tongue darted out to moisten his pouty lips. Smiling to herself, she angled the showerhead to let the spray fondle her soaked entrance with watery fingers.

Resuming her position against the tile surface, she once again slid her fingers back inside. Inner muscles clenched against her digits, filling the need for her husband's cock. Watery fingers continued massaging her sex, creating ripples of pleasure that started at the point of impact and quickly spread throughout her body.

Closing her eyes, she voiced her thoughts in a hushed tone saying, "I'm imagining your cock inside of me. Can you imagine it too?"

Her husband's only reply was a slow nod as he watched his naughty minx. Curving her fingers, she found the spot inside her sex that would push her towards the impending orgasm that was building. Her pussy tightened as her fingers continued pumping wildly. Deeper… harder… her sex clenched as her entire body shook when the orgasm hit.

"Oh God!" she moaned, relishing the subsiding ripples that shimmered over her heated skin.

Ian leaned forward to kiss her trembling lips, but she stopped him with a hand to his chest.

"Asa—"

"Wash yourself," she ordered, handing him the sponge and body wash.

"I need you," he groaned, glancing down at his angry member.

"You'll have me soon enough," she grinned wickedly. "Now… *wash.*"

Ian didn't have to be told again. With desperate movements, he washed, then quickly dried off. He reached for Asa, but she stepped out of reach, took the offered towel, and dried herself. Like a predator admiring his dinner, he watched Asa's deliberate motions as she patted the beaded drops from her skin with the soft cotton towel.

He couldn't help wishing he was the towel.

When she was finished, she dropped the towel onto the bathroom floor.

"Follow me." She grinned when he did what he was told.

This game she could definitely get used to.

"Lie in the middle of the bed."

Maneuvering himself into position, he watched as she walked to the dresser, opened the top drawer, and pulled out a long red silk scarf. He had given her the expensive item last year after he had noticed her admiring it at a local boutique in Colorado.

"Are you ready?" she purred.

Taking a deep breath, he inquired, "Am I ready for what?"

Her almond-shaped eyes narrowed playfully.

"What are you going to do to me?" the man gulped.

"Put your hands up above your head and cross them at the wrist," she instructed, running the scarf between her fingers, enjoying the silk and the anticipation in her husband's blue depths. "Perfect."

Kneeling on the mattress beside his torso, she wrapped the fabric around Ian's thick wrists. Quickly tying one end of it in a knot and attaching the other end to the headboard, she sat back on her haunches and admired her work.

One curious brow hitched to his hairline as he gauged her mood.

"Now that you have me in such a compromising position, what are you planning to do to me?"

A Cheshire cat grin spread across her face making him regret asking the question.

With a quick, graceful motion, she straddled him, placing both hands on his heaving chest and plucking at his beaded nipples. His entire body tensed as she ran her fingers through the light smattering of hair decorating his muscular chest. She felt his cock flex against her butt, making her sex dampen. Playfully, she leaned forward and gave his nipple a slow, wet glide with her tongue. His cock flexed again.

"Go lower," he urged, tugging at the scarf.

She hoped she had tied it tight enough to keep him from pulling free. Her husband had always been fit. He lifted weights and jogged often to stay that way. She, on the other hand, disliked anything strenuous except this.

"Come on, stop playing around and put me out of my misery."

In retaliation to his plea, she bit his nipple and then sucked the tip to ease the slight pain she had caused.

"No more talking."

Immediately, he stilled. When he thought she'd continue to torture him, she finally moved… lower.

Almost to the end of his rope, he watched in awe as skilled hands moved over his body, over his pecs, across his abs, through the trail of dark hair that led to his rock-hard member, but his mischievous wife totally avoided touching where he needed her most.

"Hey! If I have to rip this damn scarf in two to get inside of you, I will," he warned, blue fire dancing in his gaze, voice deep with desire. "Stop punishing me."

"*Shh,*" she winked and went back to exploring his body.

At last, the little minx settled between his legs. Her warm breath warmed his member and amplified his need to have her. Every pliant inch of her.

"You are a work of art, Ian Granger," Asa complimented, taking his heavy cock in both of her slender hands.

Instinctively, he wrapped his fingers around the wrought iron rods of the headboard to suppress the need to abandon the game and just take her.

"So masculine," she whispered to herself, a small smile brightening her beautiful features.

His entire body stilled as she began stroking his hard length. An appreciative moan escaped her chest as his cock extended another inch. Unable to keep up the charade of not being as turned on as him, she licked the slit of the engorged cockhead humming against the wide mushroom-shaped head. Ian watched with a pained expression as she took it into her mouth; heat spread through him immediately as she began a steady sucking rhythm on just the bulbous top.

"Damn," he growled, bucking up against her mouth, trying to make her take him a little bit, "Deeper, baby…."

Exhilarated by her newfound power, she nipped the head, making him yelp.

"Stop. Talking."

That did it. The last of his restraint snapped along with the delicate silk material of his seductress's scarf.

"My scarf!" Asa complained through gritted teeth.

"I'll buy you another one," he crooned, grasping her and pushing her onto her back. With speed he didn't know he possessed, he grabbed her hands, pulled them over her head, and held them immobile. "I'm sorry about the damn electricity, but I can't take being so close to you and not having you."

Her lips parted to say something, but he continued.

"I need you, *now*."

In desperation, he sealed their mouths together. His kisses were demanding, harsh, and overwhelming. On a soft whimper, Ian slipped past her defenses and plundered her with aggressive nips to her mouth and languishing lashes against her tongue.

"Ian," her moans were swallowed by his frenzied assault, and he kissed her as if he'd never gotten enough of her, and that made her smirk.

"What is it?" He paused to look at her flushed face. "Why are you smirking?"

No answer.

"This turns you on… doesn't it?"

The glimmer in her eyes spoke volumes.

"God, I love you," he proclaimed in a hushed voice as he began a quick trail of wet kisses from her chin to her left breast.

Asa remained silent but gave him a mischievous grin.

"You bit me earlier," he reminded, his raspy voice turned her on even more, and then he took her nipple between his teeth and lightly bit down. Her back arched as he sucked the entire areola into his mouth and began a hard suckling that made her tremble. "Tell me how much you want me, Asa."

"I want you so much I hurt from it," she panted, grabbing a fistful of his hair and securing him in place.

Fuck! His wife was such a wildcat.

"What do you want me to do to this amazing body of yours?" he interrogated, moving to the next breast and suckling it in a similar fashion.

Silence.

"If you don't tell me now, I'm gonna jerk myself off and go to sleep."

Her eyes widened with shock.

"Do you want me to stop?"

"No." She held him securely by the shoulders, unable to form a coherent thought that didn't include them joined at the groin.

"Tell me what you want... what you need," he ordered sternly.

"I want you to fuck me," she growled seductively, eyes glowing wildly.

"No more teasing, right?"

"No more teasing, I promise." She kissed the side of his neck. "But I want to be in control."

He studied her for a brief moment before asking, "How do you want me?"

"On your back," she stated, and when he didn't move, she clarified. "No more restraints, at least not tonight."

Giving her a quick kiss, he resumed his former position on his back and waited as she positioned herself on top of him, facing away from him.

"Spread your thighs a little wider... there you go." Maneuvering herself into position, her ass against his chest, she grinned.

"Are we gonna try... *sixty-nine*?"

Please say yes! Please say yes!

Her entire face heated as she answered, "Yup!"

"Where did you learn about this position?"

"I read it in one of my erotica novels," she smirked at his raised eyebrows and approving glare. "I wonder who comes up with these strange sexual terms."

"I don't know, but whoever it is, is fucking awesome!" he growled, gripping her hips and lifting her until her pussy hovered over his mouth.

Asa's face was inches from his lap and his extremely excited cock. The long, thick appendage flexed with a mind of its own, the crown of it brushing against her chin.

"Get to it, woman," he chuckled, making her flick the tip with her finger.

Always so feisty.

"Beast!" she giggled.

"Yup, but I'm your beast," he replied proudly, placing a kiss to her mound. Adjusting his arm, he wrapped it around her rounded hips at his chest, securing her against him. His face nuzzled between her spread thighs as he pulled her closer to his awaiting mouth. The scent of her arousal increased his desire tenfold, making his cock lengthen another impossible inch.

Her much smaller body squirmed into place as the top of her thighs ended up touching the top of Ian's muscular shoulders. Lifting his head, he used his free hand to spread her lower lips wide, allowing his mouth to fasten over her labia. Asa gasped her approval. Without any direction from him, she captured his cock and devoured it with deep sucks that made his hard member bump the back of her throat.

"Holy shit," he moaned at the knowledge his wife could take his entire steely erection into her mouth. Giving as good as he got, he used his tongue to rub the swollen nub at the apex of her thighs until she began to tremble against his glistening lips. "Damn, you taste like heaven."

Her only response was to quicken her actions. He, in turn, did the same. The more he sucked and licked, the deeper she took him. Of their own accord, his toes curled, reminding him that he was near the edge of release.

Needing her to come with him, he breached her sodden entrance with two thick fingers, curving them to rub her inner walls, finding the spot to drive her crazy as well. Instantly, her muscles began to clench, and her body stiffened as she began to come on his mouth. The intensity of it made him cry out as he continued sucking her clit with desperate tugs. Hot jets of come filled her still-sucking mouth as she swallowed every drop.

"Holy shit!" he wheezed against her sex, pushing her body forward until her pussy was lined up to his still-hard erection. "I need to be inside of you."

Asa smirked. "Have you been taking Viagra or something?" she teased, surprised he was still ready to go.

"Not Viagra," he chuckled. "I'm taking a new aphrodisiac." Her eyes narrowed suspiciously. "It's called 'Asa.' And the only side effect it has is that it leaves you needing more."

That one definitely earned him an eye roll. Gently, he entered her hot entrance. The pleasure of filling her completely in one long smooth glide made him hiss.

"You're so tight," he announced too loudly. "Have I told you how much I love that you've started taking the pill?"

As he entered her, the electricity came on, illuminating the cozy space and allowing him to see her body more clearly. *His wife was stunning.*

Asa purred as she rose to her knees and began to move up and down his shaft, the sight of her delicious ass filling his gaze made his balls tighten, and he prayed to last a few minutes longer.

"What's this position called?" she asked, grinding against his pelvis on a downward stroke.

Closing his eyes to hold off his orgasm, he mumbled, "Reverse cowgirl."

She laughed a seductive sound that made him even more desperate to come.

"Seriously? Who makes up these names?"

"I don't know," he whispered, hands gripping her hips as he began to slam against her, the movement making her look like she was actually riding a horse. "I can't last much longer."

"I'm coming," she hissed through clenched teeth, her entire body shaking from the force of her release.

Five or six strokes later, he emptied himself deep inside of her clenching passage. Bliss blanketed him as she eased off and turned around to snuggle on top of his panting chest. He hugged her tightly, enjoying her breasts as they smashed against him.

"Give me a few minutes, and we'll go again," he told, placing a chaste kiss to her forehead.

Asa grinned and began to speak when her words were cut off by Adam's hungry cry coming through the baby monitor.

"I'll give him his bottle." Quickly, he arranged her on the mattress and covered her with the comforter. "I'll be right back. You, my little wildcat, relax."

He went to the bathroom, and she heard the shower turn on briefly. A few minutes later, he reemerged, wearing a pair of loose-fitting gray sweatpants and a white t-shirt. It should be illegal to look so amazing in such simple clothes. He left for Adam's room without disturbing her.

Turning onto her stomach, she listened as her husband's voice came through the monitor.

"Hey, little guy. What are you doing up so late? Mommy and Daddy were getting it on, and you interrupted."

Asa's face instantly reddened at the words being spoken to their son. Thank goodness he was too young to understand. Adam's happy cooing sounds made her smile, followed by a fuss that told his father to hurry up with the grub.

"Wait," Ian spoke softly. "First things first… " a playful gasp preceded a surprised, "*Woowee*, son. Have you been going out for rib-eye when I'm not looking? You better not have. *Good grief!* This stuff is toxic."

The sound of a diaper being changed made her laugh into the pillow. She knew how much Ian hated changing diapers. Adam laughed too.

"Here ya go," Ian's deep baritone soothed both she and Adam. "This is formula. It's horrible, but soon you'll have more teeth, and I can make you all kinds of culinary delights instead of giving you those jars of... *sh*... stuff. This week I'm practicing making mother sauces."

Asa snorted as her husband spoke about his third love: cooking. "Mommy is listening to us right now, and she's thinking Daddy is crazy because he loves talking about food almost as much as he loves her and you."

Another smile settled over her as she listened to Adam slurping his formula hungrily. When he was finished, Ian patted his back and was rewarded with three loud manly burps.

"There ya go," her husband encouraged. "Real men burp like construction workers, loud and caveman-ish. Girls don't understand, so if you burp in front of Mommy, remember to say 'excuse me,' or she gets annoyed."

She recognized the sound of fabric rustling as Ian sat in the rocking chair beside Adam's crib.

"What would you like for me to sing to you?" he asked in a low tone, then paused. "I know. I'll sing you Mommy's favorite song."

Clearing his throat, he began.

"Lately I've been, I've been losing sleep, Dreaming about the things that we could be...."

She loved Ian's voice. Almost as much as she loved the rest of him. He could have been a professional singer if he wanted, but instead, he settled for singing to them. Approximately twenty minutes later, the door to their bedroom opened.

A shy smile played at his lips, and her chest tightened. *No one should love another person as much as she loved him.*

"I thought you'd be asleep."

Throwing back the covers to expose her naked body to his appreciative gaze, all she could say was, "Come here, Daddy. I'm ready for round two."

Chapter Thirteen

Two and a half years later…

"You got the job?" Asa waited on pins and needles as Ian closed the door behind him.

He walked toward her… stalked her, actually grabbed her by the nape, and kissed her wickedly.

"Yup," he smirked, using his tongue to trace the contours of her slender neck. "I'm the new sous chef for The Capital Grille," his announcement filled with excitement.

"That's an incredible restaurant," she interjected as he held her close. "I'm so proud of you."

"Thanks." He kissed her on the lips lingering when he heard her breath hitch. "Where's Adam?"

"Our parents took him for the weekend."

"How could both sets of grandparents take our kid?" he teased, sitting on the nearest dining chair and tugging her onto his lap. "Did they cut him in two? They better not have cut him in two."

Swiftly, she stood before he could get a better grip on her and slapped away his groping hands as she said, "Dinner is ready. Go wash your hands, and I'll set the table."

"You cooked?"

Asa had been working overtime at the gallery for the last few weeks, getting her exhibit of photographs ready for the public, and the creative director of *National Wildlife Magazine*, who she hoped would love her work enough to offer her a permanent position of a photojournalist at their new headquarters in Denver.

Their little family had recently moved back to their hometown of Denver after he had graduated from culinary school. At the moment, they lived in a quaint two-bedroom townhouse in the heart of the city that was close to both of their jobs. It wasn't their dream place, but their parents were only thirty minutes away and could help with Adam when things got too busy.

"Yes," she grinned, looking a bit nervous. "Go wash your hands."

"I was planning on making dinner," he admitted looking at his wife's exhausted expression. "You haven't been yourself lately. You need to slow down, my little wildcat."

For the past few weeks, Ian had been worried. Asa had complained about being fatigued, and the fact she was seldom hungry added to his anxiety. It had gotten to the point where he had to practically force her to eat. His wife had never been the sturdiest of women, and he always felt responsible for her welfare even though she often argued that he smothered her.

"Is everything all right?"

"Uh-huh," she hummed, avoiding eye contact.

"Are you sure?" he prodded anxiously.

"Ian," she rolled her eyes. "Dinner is going to get cold if you don't get a move on."

"Okay," he complied, disappearing down the hallway.

Asa's stomach was tied up in nervous knots as she waited for Ian to return.

"Have a seat," she encouraged, waiting for him to sit. His suspicious blue stare made her even more uncomfortable. "I hope you're hungry."

"I'm starving," he keened, adjusting his chair. "What did you make?"

Asa was almost as good a cook as he was. She loved helping him with new recipes, unlike Adam, who was going through a stage of only wanting macaroni and cheese, hot dogs, French fries, and salmon. He couldn't figure out where the hell the salmon came from.

She placed his plate in front of him and then hers as she sat. Curiously, he examined their meal which looked just as delicious as it smelled. Baby lamb chops, glazed baby carrots, baby zucchini, baby corn, and small red-skinned new potatoes.

"Looks great," he grinned, still examining the meal. "Why is everything on my plate so *small*?"

Asa's hands were clenched tightly, her knuckles turning white.

"I have something to tell you."

His posture stiffened as he eyed her warily.

"Out with it, Asa," he stated firmly. "I'm starting to worry."

"I'm pregnant," she blurted, eyes fixed on her plate.

His mouth dropped and stayed open for a long moment.

"How did that happen?"

Her eyes narrowed.

"I mean… I know how it happened, but… but, you're on the pill."

"Remember, last month; I forgot to get my prescription refilled. I've been so busy with the exhibit and working at the gallery and with Adam and the move back to Colorado—"

Ian grabbed her and kissed her until they both couldn't breathe.

"See," she panted, glancing down at her flat tummy. She whimpered. "This is what happens when you kiss me like that. I know it's a shock. We haven't discussed having another child. You're starting a new job. We're living in this tiny place—"

Kissing her again, he excitedly confessed, "I can't wait to see you carrying our daughter."

"Daughter?" She swiped away a lone tear. "How do you know it's a daughter?"

"We already have an amazing son," he informed as he took her hands in his. "A daughter that looks just like you would be incredible."

"How are we going to afford another child?" she inquired, relaxing a bit. "We are barely making ends meet as it is."

"We'll make it work," he comforted, kissing her once again. Her body stiffened as she pushed him away and ran down the hallway to the bathroom, hand clamped over her mouth, a haggard expression on her pale face.

Ahh! The joys of pregnancy.

Three months later…

"Is he asleep?" Ian asked, looking up from his electronic tablet as she entered their bedroom.

She tried to smile but didn't have the energy to.

"Finally," Asa gasped.

"Why are you out of breath? Did you go jogging… hold on," he paused. "Jogging is the last thing you would do."

"Ha! Ha!" she mocked, taking off her robe and climbing into bed with him as he lifted the comforter. Wrapping her arms around his waist, she rested her head on his chest. "I'm tired, that's all."

"Have you been taking your prenatal vitamins?"

"Yes, I have. Your three-year-old spy… aka… our son, has been monitoring me regularly. I think he should either become a spy or a private investigator when he grows up," she laughed against his chest.

Leaning over, he kissed her forehead and noticed a purplish bruise on her upper arm and another one on her wrist.

"How did that happen?"

Looking at the spots, she answered with a yawn.

"It must have been while I was hanging my photographs at the gallery. I didn't realize they were there."

"You have to be careful." He turned off the tablet, rested it on the nightstand, and adjusted himself so they were looking into each other's eyes, dark brown to blue. "I got an offer to help cater a rotary club banquet with Brian."

"Brian is doing well with his management properties. I didn't know he wanted to start a catering business as well," she stated, tracing a circular pattern around his nipple, making him squirm.

The covers above his groin instantly tented, and she stopped.

"I'm too tired," she giggled, discontinuing her motions.

"Yeah," he agreed, tightening his hold on her. "He knows of a few more local businesses interested in catering their holiday functions."

"That's great," she said, closing her eyes. "I'm so proud of you…"

And her words slurred as she drifted off to sleep.

Ian hated hospitals, hated them with a fiery passion that burned in his soul. It had started when he was in the third grade and got bitten by a stray dog while walking home. His mind had blocked out most of that terrifying event, but he remembered being in the ambulance surrounded by strangers because his parents were both at work in the city.

Asa was walking with him too, but because they were not related, she wasn't allowed to ride in the ambulance with him. Instead, she and her parents followed behind and stayed with him the entire time until his parents got there.

That was the last time he had seen the inside of any hospital.

"I'm looking for my wife, Asa Granger," he huffed, trying to catch his breath and contain his concern.

The nurse looked up the name on her computer.

"She's in exam room three. I'll take you to her."

"Is she okay?" Ian huffed, his mind swirling uncontrollably.

"The doctor is checking her out right now," the nurse informed with a soothing half-smile. "We'll know more after he's finished."

"All right." He squeezed his car keys tightly in his fist as he followed the kind woman.

"Here we are," the nurse nodded, pulling back the curtain revealing his wife and the consulting doctor."

He glanced around the space and took a deep breath before stepping forward. Inside his belly, there were pterodactyls playing keep-away with his intestines. It was all he could do not to lose his lunch right there and then.

"Ian," Asa smiled weakly, bringing back to the situation at hand. "Dr. Khan, this is my husband, Ian."

Without hesitation, he shook the man's outstretched hand. Dr. Khan was a tall, lean man with kind eyes and a warm demeanor. Ian assumed he was a few years older than his parents, but he honestly could not tell. All he knew was that his wife trusted and respected the man, and that was enough for him.

"It's nice to meet you, Mr. Granger." Dr. Khan gave a friendly grin.

"You too," he mumbled, hugging his wife like she might turn into vapor and evaporate.

"I've known Dr. Khan since I was five when we moved here from Detroit."

Dr. Khan smiled, revealing two perfect rows of white teeth.

"You have an amazing wife, young man, but she's a stubborn one. Don't let her bully you," he teased.

The other man really did know her well.

"How is she?"

"Dr. Khan just got here," Asa added, trying to calm his agitated state.

"Asa was catching me up on Adam, and your budding culinary career," his wife's Oncologist made small talk which actually took his mind off where he was.

Their easy banter calmed his nerves... a bit.

"What happened?" His question was directed towards Asa, who was currently hooked to an IV and automatic blood pressure machine.

"I felt dizzy," she mumbled. "Miriam overreacted and brought me here."

"Good." He kissed her cheek and then smoothed her hair away from her face. Again he asked, "How is she? How's the baby?"

"She's dehydrated, and I have a feeling she's anemic," Dr. Khan educated with a furrowed brow. "I took some blood samples, and we're waiting for the results. I have to see a few other patients, but I'll be back as soon as I get the results of your wife's blood screens."

"Thanks," he said, shaking the man's hand again.

As Dr. Khan left the small examination room, Ian turned to Asa and asked, "Is this the first time you've had a dizzy spell?"

No answer. Sadly, he knew what that meant.

"How long has this been going on?" he continued.

Deafening silence filled the space as they stared at each other.

"Has it been going on since New York?"

He ran a frustrated hand across his face while Asa sat looking miserable.

"Are you gonna make me continue guessing?"

After a minute or so, she finally replied, saying, "Since we've been back."

"We've been in Denver for four months," he reminded.

"I know," she mumbled below her breath as she rolled her eyes and fiddled with the blanket covering her.

"Why didn't you tell me?" Ian grilled his sad wife.

"I didn't want to worry you."

"Worry me," his voice raised an octave. "Are you serious?"

Suddenly, he began to pace.

"I'm your husband. I need to know if you're not well. You're pregnant—"

"I'm sorry," Asa whispered, and hearing those rare words stopped him in midstride. "I should have told you, but in my defense, I didn't want you to worry about me when you've got so much going on with the new catering business you and Brian have been doing on the side."

When her eyes welled, he couldn't help the protectiveness that settled over him. Asa rarely cried, and the sight of her showing remorse was more than he could stomach.

"Sweetheart," he tried comforting her as he sat on a chair beside her bed. "Don't cry; you know I can't stand seeing you cry."

"I'm sorry, Ian," she sniffled, and he was undone.

"I'll see if I can change to the daytime shift at the restaurant, so I can help out at night," he consoled, wiping away the warm rivulets now trickling down her cheeks.

"What about the catering business?" she countered, trying to contain a sob.

"I'll tell Brian to limit events to once a month." He kissed her gently on the lips, lingering longer than necessary. "Don't hide things from me anymore."

Judging from the gruffness in his voice, she knew it wasn't a request.

"I won't," she pulled him closer and kissed him back. "How are my parents doing with Adam?"

Laughing, he told her that her Dad said he needed a nap, but her mom was having a great time teaching the precocious three-year-old how to make her famous chocolate chip cookies.

"That's the first thing she taught me to cook as well," Asa giggled.

"You know how to make your mom's cookies?" Blue eyes studied her intensely.

"Uh-huh," she confessed, kissing him again.

"Why didn't you tell me?" his eyes narrowed playfully.

"Because I didn't want you asking me to marry you when we were ten," her tone was mocking but sweet.

"Good thinking," he agreed as Dr. Khan reentered the room, a concerned expression on his face.

"What's wrong?" she asked first.

"You are definitely anemic, and the blood tests show an elevated lymphocyte count, which given your medical history, worries me. I requested a full blood panel workup and will know more once I receive the results. I want you to come to my office tomorrow."

"All right." Asa's unreadable mask suddenly transformed her face into something much more nerve-racking.

"My receptionist will call you with the time," Dr. Khan gave a small, forced smile. "Go ahead and get dressed. Here's a prescription for iron supplements, along with one to increase your appetite. You're thinner than you should be."

"But the baby is okay?" Slender hands rubbed her slight baby bump protectively.

Dr. Khan's face beamed.

"The baby is doing great. Everything is progressing nicely, and the medicine I gave you won't affect it at all."

They both released relieved breaths.

"We'll see you tomorrow, doctor." Ian took the prescriptions and got Asa's clothes and purse from the hook on the wall. "Thanks again."

Dinner came together in record time. He, of course, cooked while Adam helped set the table, and his wife sat and watched her hardworking men tend to her every need. The little boy even got their drinks, wiped the kitchen counters, and carefully loaded the dirty dishes into the dishwasher so his father didn't have to. Ian smiled at how their son had so much energy in comparison to his parents, who looked haggard and exhausted.

Twenty-five minutes later, they all were sitting at the dining table: he and Adam were eating with gusto, his wife not eating at all.

"Asa, you have to eat something," Ian pressed, watching his wife push her food around her plate with her fork.

What was she supposed to do? Lie and say she felt great and could have run a marathon without breaking a sweat. Honestly, all she had the energy to do was trudge upstairs and collapse on their bed. She didn't even know if she had the strength to do that.

Everything hurt: her body, her mind, and her only solace were watching her adorable guys take care of her. She knew Ian was a worrier as well as Adam. They were constantly asking if she needed something, but she kept insisting that she was fine. She wasn't fine, not by a long shot.

"Aren't you hungry, Mommy?" Adam asked before taking a bite of the homemade macaroni and cheese with mixed vegetables and cubed ham.

Their kid was such a great eater. Even as a baby, he had the appetite of a much older child. Now, he was almost to the point of eating like his father. What would they do when he became a teenager? They'd probably need to get second jobs just to feed him.

"Take a bite," Ian ordered with a frown, snapping her out of her musings. "If you don't eat at least half of your dinner, you can't get dessert."

That did it. She began eating and, to her husband's astonishment, cleaned the small portion from her plate in less than two minutes.

"What's for dessert?" she beamed when she was finished, her eyes sparkling under the dangling pendant lights overhead at the mere mention of something sweet.

"I'll get it!" Adam ran to the kitchen and returned with a small plastic container.

With determination, he pried off the lid to reveal a dozen and a half of her mother's chocolate chip cookies. His airy giggle made her laugh.

"My mom usually gives us two dozen. Where are the rest of them?" Asa looked at her spouse, the guilty expression making her chuckle. She already knew the answer.

"We had to make sure it was a good batch," Adam chimed in, in his father's defense.

"Whose idea was it to *test* the batch?" she folded her arms across her chest.

"Daddy's," Adam informed, handing her one of the soft cookies.

"Of course it was."

It was Ian's turn to tuck Adam into bed, but the boy wanted his mother to do it. Admittedly, he was a little hurt by the request, but he understood and stepped aside. Asa, of course, was happy to take over.

"That didn't take very long," he chuckled, patting the mattress beside him as Asa entered the room, closing the door behind her.

"He must have been exhausted," she smiled as she snuggled beside him, enjoying his warmth. Inhaling deeply, she filled her lungs with the scent of Ian's body wash and his natural essence. "You smell delicious."

"Do I?" he blushed.

In response, she licked his sensitive nipple and ran an unhurried hand across his tight abs.

"You feel just as good," she suddenly straddled his waist, and instantly his cock was at full salute.

"Are you sure you're up for this?"

With an arrogant chuckle, she teased, saying, "*You* are definitely *up* for this."

Boldly, Asa leaned forward and kissed his full lips as she began lifting the hem of her *Denver Broncos* nightshirt. Ian halted her movement, causing curiosity to fill her.

"What's wrong?" his wife sighed.

"We have to see Dr. Khan in the morning," he reminded, pulling her against his chest to a lying position with her head nestled on his pecs. The soft fragrance of roses surrounded him and tickled his nose. "His receptionist called. We have to go in for eleven."

She tried to say something, but he answered before she could speak.

"My mom is going to stay here with Adam. She asked if we wanted her to take him for the night, but I said I had to ask you first."

"Would you mind if he didn't spend the night?"

His curious gaze made her clarify.

"I was thinking we could spend the afternoon together," Asa begged. "Maybe see a movie… get some lunch. You took the day off, right?"

Ian nodded.

"What do you think?" she added.

Hugging her tighter, he said, "Sounds good to me." Then he gently rolled her over onto her back, settled between her spread thighs, and announced with a breathy sigh, "Now… I think I was just about to have my way with you."

Chapter Fourteen

Dr. Khan's office, located on the third floor of the hospital, was tastefully decorated in shades of blue, dark brown, and ivory. In the center of the space, there were two long brown sofas back-to-back. The perimeter of the room was lined with single chairs, each being separated by metal and glass end tables decorated with a variety of contemporary magazines.

In the far back, an area for the children was set up with books, games, puzzles, and a television set that played *PBS* educational programs. The entire place was calm and peaceful and giving him hives. Nervously, he thumbed through a *Field & Stream* magazine as Asa did the same with a *Cosmopolitan*.

"Are you nervous?" she whispered so only he could hear.

"Aren't you?" he frowned, not caring who else saw.

As she was about to answer, the nurse's voice came from the doorway leading to the back of the facility.

"Asa Granger?"

Slowly, they both stood and made their way in the nurse's direction.

"Hi, that's me," Asa smiled warmly.

"It's nice to see you, Mrs. Granger… Mr. Granger," the nurse smiled back. "Dr. Khan is waiting for you in his office. Please, follow me."

Asa subtly took his hand in hers. Her palms were slightly sweaty, reminding him that his wife was more nervous than she let on. That knowledge made him feel worse.

They entered the third door on the right of the hallway and waited for the nurse to leave before he asked, "Why do you think he wants to see us?"

Her only response was shrugging her slender shoulders.

"Good morning, Asa. Ian, how are you two this morning?" Dr. Khan greeted them as they entered his office.

"Nervous," Ian blurted, then immediately wished he hadn't.

Dr. Khan grinned but didn't respond. That was never a good sign. Asa knew the doctor well, too well. And like everyone else, he had tells; tells that someone as perceptive as her would eventually decipher given enough time.

"I've been reviewing the results of your tests," Dr. Khan cleared his throat once, twice, and then he reached for his bottled water and took two small sips.

Tell number two.

"I even had them run a second time to be certain—"

That cemented it.

"Say it," Asa interrupted, her heartbeat thumping in her ears. "I already know."

"You already know… *what*?" Ian sat straighter. Asa, on the other hand, stared down at their intertwined fingers. "Dr. Khan, please tell me what the hell is going on."

"It's back," she blurted in a low tone. "My leukemia is back."

In shock, he glanced between the doctor and his wife.

"Is she right?" he demanded, feeling the bile rise in his esophagus.

Dr. Khan nodded and slowly removed his reading glasses, resting them carefully on his desk.

"Damn it!" Ian's temper flared, and for a brief second, he wanted to smash everything breakable around him. "She gets

biannual check-ups! Hell! She's been in remission since she was eleven! *Fuckin' shit!*"

"It's still in the early stages," Dr. Khan soothed as he opened his calendar and began to thumb through its pages. "We can start chemotherapy immediately."

"No," Asa mumbled, holding back her desire to run screaming from the room.

"Did you say something, Asa?" Dr. Kahn tensed.

"I said *no*," she replied more forcefully, that unreadable mask once again showing. "No chemo until after the baby is born."

"Asa, you have six more months left of your pregnancy." Perplexed, the doctor sat back in his chair, the age lines on his face even more pronounced now. The cancer could spread—"

"I did some research last night, and everything that I read said pregnant women should not have chemo," she verbally challenged the man she viewed as a second father, as well as a trusted friend.

"You are young," Dr. Khan added reassuringly. "You've got a healthy reproductive system. You can try again after—"

"No," she proclaimed again, only louder. "I'm not terminating this pregnancy."

Suddenly she stood, avoiding his wide-eyed stare, and picked up her purse.

"I'll keep taking all of the vitamins and anti-nausea medicine. I'll even force myself to gain weight if I have to, but I will not sacrifice this baby."

And with that, she turned and headed for the door.

Ian and Dr. Khan watched as she left in stunned speechlessness.

They pretended everything was fine as they took Adam to *The Cherry Cricket* for burgers, fries, and shakes, then went to see a Disney movie at the dollar movie theatre. They even forgot to be angry with each other as they played and joked with their son, but at the end of the day, when Adam had gone to bed, and they were lying in bed in silence, it began.

"How could you make such a monumental decision without discussing it with me first?" he huffed as he stared up at the ceiling.

"It's my body and my decision," Asa stated matter-of-factly, making him even angrier.

"That's complete and utter bullshit, and you know it," he mimicked her tone.

"I'm not losing the baby, and that's the end of it," she said, turning away to face the opposite direction.

A long moment passed before he growled, "I think you should have the chemo."

"I said no, and that's final," she mumbled.

Unable to be near her any longer, Ian grabbed his pillow and headed to the living room to sleep on the couch.

"Where are you going?" she called after him, but the slamming door was his only response.

Three days later, they still weren't speaking. Occasionally, they would let the other person know about important events or information, but other than that, their relationship was strained. Ian had been sleeping on the sofa while she tossed and turned over her decision every night alone in their bed. Her face was pale, her eyes bloodshot and puffy due to crying every night, and the anti-nausea medicine didn't seem to be helping.

Still, true to her word… she ate. Even though nothing stayed down, she took her medicine and vitamins regularly and made sure to drink supplement shakes throughout the day when her stomach settled. Crackers and ginger ale were her two new best friends. She carried them in her purse wherever she went.

"Mommy, Mommy!" Adam shouted as she picked him up from her mother-in-law's house.

"Hey, big guy!" Asa greeted warmly, hugging him and kissing the top of his dark head. Blue eyes like his daddy shone up at her melting her foul mood. "What have you and Grandma been doing?"

"Making dinner," the little boy made a face.

"What did Grandma Ramona make this time?" She made a face too.

"It kinda looks like soup," he whispered close to her ear when she bent. "But it doesn't smell like soup."

"Umm… what does it smell like?" his mother grimaced.

"Yuck," he wrinkled his nose, making her laugh.

"C'mon in, Asa," Mrs. Granger waved at her from the front doorway. The red and white checkered apron she wore was covered with flour and other stuff.

"I thought you said she was making soup?" she questioned her son warily. "Why is Grandma covered in flour?"

"She was trying to make it thicker," he said with a strange lilt to his voice that reminded her of… her.

He may not have been hers biologically, but he was definitely her little boy.

"I see," Asa smirked. "I guess we better go and taste it."

Knowing what was to come, her stomach began to roil at the thought of ingesting what would probably be food poisoning in a bowl. She loved her mother-in-law dearly, but love had its limits. Especially when dealing with questionable dishes.

"*Oh, no!* The soup is getting too thick!" Ramona shouted with disappointment. "Take a look. I don't want to throw it away. Maybe you could help me salvage it."

"Great," Asa mocked below her breath. "We wouldn't want that to happen."

Taking her son's hand, they made their way back to the house.

"Whatever you do, don't eat it, Mom."

"Okay," she agreed with a devilish wink.

"Should we tell her that it doesn't smell good?" Adam frowned at the idea of hurting his grandmother's feelings.

"No," she replied, shaking her head. "We don't want her to feel bad."

"Then what do we do?"

"Don't worry," Asa quickly formulated a plan. "I've got an idea."

An hour and a half later, they were sitting all together at the dining table: Ramona, Jackson, her father-in-law, and she and Adam. The delicious aroma wafted around the large space making everyone's mouth water.

"I see I'm just in time for dinner," Ian's voice startled them all.

"Yes, dear," Ramona keened, motioning for him to sit beside his wife. "You've got perfect timing."

"Yeah, Son," his dad gulped loudly, a curious look on his face. "Join us. We were about to *taste* your mother's mouthwatering meal."

Ian chuckled to himself and sat next to his grinning wife.

"It smells good," Ian frowned, but unfortunately, he had fallen for the old smells good trick one too many times.

"Dig in," his mother encouraged everyone while she dished out Adam's serving.

Reluctantly, everybody took a small sip from their spoons, even his mom.

"Holy crap," his father mumbled, taking another tentative bite and then a third. "This is delicious!" Then he took a thick slice of bread from the bread basket and dipped it into the steaming broth.

"It is, isn't it?" his mother's face beamed.

From the corner of his eye, he saw when Asa winked at Adam, and Adam smiled back.

"It is really tasty, Ramona," Asa praised, then took a slice of bread as well.

"Is this a new recipe, Mom?" Ian dug in too.

Ramona swallowed before informing, "I was trying out something new, Italian wedding soup."

"Oh!" Ian began chewing on a tender, well-seasoned mini meatball.

"It was keeping warm on the stove when Asa came to get Adam," her voice lowered. "I asked Asa to taste it to make sure there was enough salt in it." She paused and patted his wife's hand reassuringly. "Being pregnant, she got dizzy and accidentally knocked the pot into the sink."

"I felt so bad about it that I recreated the soup," Asa blushed. "To make up for wasting the entire pot… I'm sure it would have been an amazing soup."

His anger dissipated like mist as he watched his amazing wife.

Halfway through dinner, there was a knock on the door.

"I'll get it," his father announced, resting his spoon beside his third helping of Italian wedding soup. The older gentleman left quickly, returning with a scowl of epic proportions on his face.

"What's wrong?" his mother probed, putting down her spoon. "Who was at the door, Jackson?"

Jackson stepped aside to reveal a familiar blonde that could be seen behind him, glancing nervously at each staring face.

"I'm sorry for interrupting dinner," the woman stated meekly, voice quivering.

"*Misty?*" Ian almost choked on his noodle.

When Asa's eyes narrowed, he knew he'd have to deal with Misty before Asa handled her. It would not be a pretty sight if his wife got to her first. He was positive there would be blows.

"What are you doing here?" he asked the obvious.

Misty ignored him and glanced around the table; her eyes landed on Adam.

"Is that—"

"Adam," he interrupted.

"Hi, Adam," his biological mother purred, not surprised when Adam scooted his chair closer to Asa. "You've gotten so big."

"That tends to happen with children." Asa wiped her mouth with her napkin and hugged Adam protectively against her. "Especially after three years."

"Mommy?" Adam's voice lowered. "Who is this?"

Before Asa could answer, Ian stood, grabbed Misty by the arm, and walked her outside to the front porch.

"You've got some nerve showing up here," he snarled once they were out of earshot, unable to control his temper any longer.

"I'm sorry—"

"Yeah, you are sorry," he agreed sarcastically as he began pacing the length of the area, hands balled into intimidating fists. "I have full custody of Adam." His pacing stopped as he stared at her, blue eyes dark with fury. "If you try any shit, I swear I'll—"

"Ian," Misty tried to touch his arm, but he pulled out of reach. "I only wanted to see my little boy."

"You saw him," the normally laid-back man practically growled. "Now go." It was then he noticed her round stomach. "You're pregnant *again*?"

"I'm four months along," she said in a hushed tone, pulling her cardigan closed to hide her belly.

A maniacal laugh escaped his mouth before he could stop it.

"Who is the baby-daddy this time?" he provoked with a lingering snarl.

"Tommy," she whispered.

"Let me guess," he sat on the nearby porch swing. "He doesn't want it or you. Is that the long and short of it?"

At a loss for words, she simply nodded.

"I feel bad for you, but that's not my problem."

"Ian, I don't have anywhere else to go," she sniffled.

"Go to your parent's house," he snapped, unable to quell the need to be rid of her.

A sigh passed her lips as she clarified, "They don't want anything to do with me."

"Gee, I wonder why?" his sarcasm was unchecked and harsh even to his own ears.

"I need some cash," she whimpered.

Immediately, his mouth gaped.

"You've got to be fuckin' kiddin' me!"

"I have nothing, Ian. I'm living in a shelter—"

"We have two thousand dollars saved," Asa's voice startled them both. "I'll meet you at the coffee shop near the boutique where you used to work tomorrow morning, nine o'clock."

And with that declaration, Asa folded her arms across her chest, thereby ending the entire horrible conversation.

"Thank you," Misty smiled shyly, then turned and quickly left.

"What the hell did you just do?" he mumbled, staring at the retreating blonde.

"Cleaning up your mess," she turned to go back inside. "As usual."

"Who was that lady at Grandma and Grandpa's house?"

Asa stilled from the nightly routine of tucking her son into bed.

"That was your biological mommy," Asa explained. "Remember I showed you her picture once."

"I have blonde hair like her," he frowned.

"Yes," she touched his tousled blonde locks with a gentle hand. "You have her blonde hair, but you have your daddy's blue eyes and his mischievous smile."

Instantly, his eyes welled.

"I don't have anything of yours?"

She grinned before explaining, "You have my temper, and my stubbornness, and most importantly... you have my love."

"I don't want her to be my mommy," Adam stiffened. "I only want you."

"You are my baby boy... no matter what... okay?" she clarified with a huge smile.

She lay beside him on his twin-sized bed, tucking his *Man of Steel* comforter around his body like a mummy the way he liked it.

"Are you going to love the new baby more than me?" Adam watched her sadly.

"Absolutely not," she hugged him tight. "I'm gonna love you both exactly the same."

"How much?" the boy finally smiled.

Without hesitation, she told, "I'm gonna love you both as much as all of the stars in the sky."

"That's a lot," he yawned sleepily.

"Yes," his mother agreed, kissing his forehead and closing her eyes. "It is a lot."

"Do you still love Daddy?"

The question startled her, but she happily admitted it as she yawned too. "Of course."

"How much?" her son asked again, blue eyes closed, fingers playing with her hair.

That was an easy question.

"More than all of the stars in the sky…"

At exactly nine a.m., Asa entered the small coffeehouse and swept the busy space with a predatory eye. Misty sat sipping a hot beverage but stopped when she saw her. Her face paled, and she clenched her fingers nervously as Asa approached.

"Hi, Asa," Misty grinned nervously.

Without sitting, she handed the woman a plain white envelope.

"Here," Asa grunted, looking down at her with murderous intent. "I managed to scrape together another five hundred. There's no more to get."

"Thanks—"

"You are not to come near me or my family again. Do you understand?"

Misty nodded.

"If you go back on your word… let's just say what I do to you won't be pleasant."

"Are you threatening me?" the blonde tensed.

"Yes, yes, I am."

Ian stared at his wife and his son's biological mother from outside the glass windows of the building. Asa's expression alone was enough to make his balls shrivel, and his chest tighten, and he wished he could hear their conversation.

When Asa exited, he stopped her with a gentle tug on her elbow.

"How did it go?" Ian pried anxiously, his stomach in knots.

But there was no answer.

"What did you say to her?" he continued, his frustration growing.

Still, there was silence.

"I know my mistake keeps coming back to bite us in the ass, but in my defense—" Stunned silence came over him as she grabbed him and kissed him ravenously.

"I love Adam," she hissed when she finally pulled away. "And I love you. Don't ever forget it."

"I won't." He pulled her closer, unable to stop his heart from clenching. "I'm sorry about the last few days."

"I'm sorry too," she sniffled. "I'm still not doing chemo. We'll have to deal with the consequences."

"I know," he tightened his grip on her. "I know."

Chapter Fifteen

Five months later…

"Adam, we've got to go!" Ian yelled from downstairs. "Mommy's gonna have this baby on the living room floor if you don't get a move on!"

Asa watched him knowingly.

"What?" he snapped.

"Women deliver babies all the time," she reminded in the middle of doing one of her Lamaze breathing techniques. "Stop taking out your anxiety on our four-year-old."

"How can you be so… *Zen* right now?" he quibbled, glancing at his watch again. "You're a month early. They'll probably have to put the baby in an incubator."

"Maybe, you should breathe," she mocked with a grin.

The uncharacteristic, miffed stare he gave made her cringe.

"Where's your suitcase?" he babbled, turning in circles like a dog chasing its tail.

"It's in the SUV, remember?" Asa chuckled, feeling sorry for her obviously discombobulated spouse. "You put it in there after our last doctor's appointment."

"I was thinking ahead; good for me," he replied sheepishly. "Did you talk to your editor?"

"I did. She knows I'm taking the full twelve weeks off for maternity leave. Then I'll work on assignments on a part-time basis until the baby is old enough to go to preschool."

"Sounds good to me," Ian inhaled deeply. "Who is gonna pick up Adam at the hospital?"

"Both sets of grandparents are going to meet us there."

"Good." He exhaled too quickly, making himself lightheaded. "I have an appointment with the contractor tomorrow. I'll call to reschedule."

"No," she admonished, shaking her head. "Ask him to meet us at the hospital to go over the final cosmetic changes to the house."

Hesitantly, he agreed with a nod.

With his swiftly growing catering business and Asa's permanent photojournalism job with *National Wildlife Magazine,* they had bought the empty one-acre lot adjacent to Asa's parent's house and were in the last stages of building their dream home. It was similar in size and style to their parents' houses but with a few less bells and whistles. Four bedrooms, three baths, and two car garage; the only things they splurged on were a state-of-the-art gourmet kitchen and a small addition to the back of the house that would act as a photography studio for both Asa and Adam. To his parent's delight, Adam had decided to follow in his mother's footsteps.

The contractor needed their final decision on the hardwood flooring and tiles for the master ensuite bathroom. Personally, he didn't care about any of it, but of course, his wife had her mind set on certain design elements.

Women.

He'd never understand them, no matter how hard he tried. They were a complete mystery. Especially his wife.

"You're working yourself into a frenzy for no reason," Asa frowned, grinding her teeth through another mind-shattering contraction.

"How are you doing, Sweetheart?" he inquired when his wife's eyes rolled to the back of her head, stayed there for several seconds, and then finally returned to their usual place.

"How do you think I'm doing, Ian?!" she barked, actually showing her teeth.

Ignoring her statement, he glanced at his watch again. If they didn't get to the hospital soon, Asa would be delivering right here on the living room floor. There was no way he was going to let that happen because, with luck, he'd be the one cleaning it up, and the idea of that was already making him gag.

"This boy is slower than molasses."

Ian sat down on the sofa, then stood, and then sat one more time. At last, Adam appeared on the stairs.

"Don't leave without me!"

"What were you doing, son?" he rose to his feet again.

"I had to get something." The little boy smirked, reminding him of Asa. Their son was also just as moody as her. "I'm ready. Let's go!"

"Are you gonna make it to the hospital?"

Please say yes… please say yes.

Instead of answering, she gave him a thumbs-up.

In less than five minutes, they were speeding to the medical facility. Ian's blood pressure was rising along with his concern. During the course of the pregnancy, she had gained a little over ten pounds, which made him and her doctors happy, but she was still very frail-looking, and exhaustion overcame her easily.

"Ian, slow down!" Asa clenched her teeth, holding back a pained yelp as another much harder contraction slammed into her. "Holy shit!" she swore and then quickly apologized to their shocked son. "I think my water just *broke!*"

Her mortified expression made him queasy.

"In our new SUV?" he whined, then clamped his lips down when he realized he had said the thought out loud. "Hold on for ten more minutes!"

"I... I..." she stammered, looking forlorn and out of her element. If there was one thing that Asa hated, it was not being in control. "I need... to..." her legs slammed together as she screamed, *"Push!"*

"Hold it!" he yelled back.

"I can't hold it!" She closed her eyes in an attempt to gain some self-control.

"Mommy is the baby coming now?" Adam gasped.

"I think so!" his mother bellowed with a strained frown.

Ian cursed a blue streak as he pulled out his cell phone and dialed 911.

"This is 911… what is the nature of your emergency?" the calm dispatcher responded, which further pissed him off.

Why was everyone else so freaking calm?

"My name is Ian Granger!" he shouted in a panic. "My wife's in labor, and we're driving to the hospital right now, but she wants to… *Push!*"

"Mr. Granger, I need you to pull over."

He immediately did as he was told.

When he was parked, he looked over at Asa, who looked in distress. *Fuck!* He wasn't used to being the rational one in their relationship.

"I'm parked at the side of South Downing Street a few blocks away from Porter Adventist Hospital."

"I need you to check your wife." The soft island accent calmed his frayed nerves.

"Check her for what?" he asked densely.

"Daddy, what's going on?" Adam questioned from the back seat.

"I'm getting help from," he paused before asking, "I'm sorry I didn't get your name."

"It's Catherine," the dispatcher stated sweetly.

"Nice to meet you, Catherine, but could you please repeat… what am I doing?"

"I need you to check if the crown is visible," the woman complied.

"Crown?" he repeated. "What would a crown be doing up my wife's—"

A low chuckle came from the other end.

"Mr. Granger, the crown of the baby's head."

"Of course." His head began to swim, but he reined it in. "Okay," he whispered.

Quickly, he opened the door and ran around to the passenger side, where Asa sat panting like she was running a marathon.

"I need to check you."

She adjusted her chair back as far as it could go, raised the hem of her dress, and, as discreetly as possible, wiggled out of her maternity panties.

"Open your legs wider," Ian instructed, listening to the dispatcher's words. "Fuck… shit… motherfucker… "

"What do you see?" Catherine queried over the line.

"I see the top of the baby's head!" he exclaimed into the cell phone, face pale, mouth dry, heart rate beating at a supersonic rate.

"I'm going to walk you through the process," Catherine soothed, her tone never faltering, and he thanked God that she was the one who answered the call.

Asa squealed again, and his eyes widened.

"What process?" he gulped; mouth as dry as a bone.

"You're going to have to deliver this baby, Mr. Granger."

Ian felt his stomach lurch.

"*Nooooo…* send an ambulance, right the hell now!"

"The ambulance is on its way, but I don't think it'll get to you in time."

"I can't do this," he huffed. "I'm not a doc—"

Suddenly, Asa grabbed his wrist and got him to look in her glistening brown eyes.

"I need you to help me… *us*… I can't do this by myself."

She took another deep breath, and he could see her pain.

Taking a few deep breaths of his own, he asked, "Ok, what do I need to do?"

"First, I need you to…"

The ride to the hospital in the back of the ambulance was cramped, to say the least, but after their recent ordeal delivering at the side of the road, nothing would ever faze them again. Thank goodness the paramedics showed up just as the baby's head popped out. Asa, as usual, was a champ: giving birth without any pain relief. He, on the other hand needed a stiff drink. Even Adam tried to help by holding the cell phone as he pretended he knew what he was doing, so their son wouldn't freak out.

"She's beautiful." Adam smiled lovingly at the little bald bundle in his mother's arms. "What are we gonna call her?"

"That's a good question. Daddy and I couldn't decide on a name," Asa admitted.

"You helped keep Daddy calm," Ian praised with a large dose of embarrassment. "If it's okay with Mommy, you could name her."

A smiling Asa added, "I think that's a wonderful idea."

"Me?" Adam blushed.

"Go ahead, sweetheart," Asa nodded encouragingly. "What do you think we should call your baby sister?"

Their son was quiet for a long time before saying, "Ava."

Their eyes narrowed as they both asked in unison, "Why Ava?"

"Because it rhymes with Asa," he grinned.

"That was one of the names on our list. I love it," Asa grinned also. "What do you think?"

Ian touched their daughter's soft cheek.

"It's perfect, but we still need a middle name." Out of the left field, he blurted, "The dispatcher's name is Catherine."

"Catherine is a nice middle name." Adam touched the baby's forehead, a look of awe on his adorable face.

"I agree. What do you think… Ava Catherine Granger?" Asa consulted the tiny entity yawning in her arms. "Ava Catherine, it is."

"Wait a minute!" Adam took off his *Spiderman* backpack and pulled a neatly wrapped package out. "This is for Ava," he said proudly. "Open it."

Ian took it from his small hand and carefully unwrapped the item. His eyes immediately welled, and his chest puffed out with fatherly pride.

"It's a collage."

Asa began to cry as she looked at the eight-and-a-half by eleven-sized picture frame displaying one small photograph of the three of them in the middle, surrounded by pictures of them solo. Taking it from his dad's hand, he said, "When we get to the hospital, we can take a picture of the four of us and replace this one in the middle."

"That is a great idea." She tugged her son closer and kissed both of his cheeks. "Have I told you how much I love you?"

"Yeah," Adam snorted. "All the time."

Chapter Sixteen

Two months later…

"It doesn't look good." Dr. Khan removed his glasses and rubbed his temples.

"It spread," Asa said, squeezing Ian's hand in hers.

"We'll start chemo as soon as possible," Dr. Khan stated without hesitation. "My office will schedule it for next week Monday. I'll have my nurse make the arrangements and call you with all of the details."

Asa agreed as she looked over at Ava sleeping in her carrier and Adam coloring in his coloring book beside her.

"How many treatments do you think I'll need?"

"We'll start with a treatment every six weeks. If we need to go more aggressive," he paused and looked down at his chart. "We'll have to wait and see."

The doctor didn't look happy.

At all.

"Thank you," Ian said, shaking his hand and going to gather up their children. "I'll make sure she takes care of herself in the meanwhile."

"I know you will," Dr. Khan stated confidently.

"Don't make me feed you, Asa," Ian studied her nauseous expression and sallow complexion. "You're gonna need your strength for the treatments."

"I know," she mumbled, taking a bite of the perfectly cooked pot roast followed by a forkful of mashed potatoes. Not even sitting at their new dining table in their new house could lift her spirit.

"Much better," he smirked, giving her a saucy wink. "Ava is eating well, too," he watched in awe as their daughter finished the last of her pumped breast milk.

Asa started sniffling for the second time in less than five minutes.

"What's wrong?"

"I won't be able to breastfeed her anymore." She stopped to wipe away a falling tear. "I'll have to pump as much as possible in the next week and freeze it."

"That's just as good," her husband replied as she shot him the look of death. "I know you wanted to breastfeed her, but don't forget we are dealing with the consequences."

"I know," Asa mumbled, taking another bite of her dinner.

Several red marks caught his attention as he studied her.

"What are those red spots on your chest and arms?"

"Those are called Petechiae." Her cheeks reddened.

"Petechiae," he mumbled, testing the word and hating it.

"They are just dark-red spots under the skin that are caused by bleeding," Asa explained. "It's normal for patients with leukemia to get them. I've gotten them before when I was little."

"*Hmm,*" he pouted, burping Ava. "You're not hungry either, son?"

"No, sir," he sniffled. "May I be excused?"

"Sure," Ian's voice lowered right before Adam ran upstairs.

"I'll go talk to him." Asa took her time standing, joints aching a little more each day. Unfortunately, her fatigue also increased on a daily basis.

"Good luck with that," he frowned.

Asa had met her match in the stubborn, mercurial five-year-old. They were so much alike that it was frightening at times. He hated to admit that their closeness sometimes made him a bit jealous.

Asa slowly opened Adam's door. Sullen and pouty, Adam lay in the middle of the dark room, looking up at the glowing plastic stars on his ceiling.

Unmoving.

Unblinking.

Asa remembered telling him about when she and Ian were kids; they would go up on their roofs and watch the skies. She hoped to do that with Adam and Ava in the near future. Of course, there would be a batch of homemade cookies involved.

"May I come in?"

"I don't want you to be sick," he said, wiping away a stream of tears with the back of his hand.

"I don't want to be sick either," she confessed, lying beside him and holding his much smaller hand. "Sometimes life doesn't work out the way you imagine." She paused, turning to look into his weepy blue eyes. "But it works out the way it is supposed to—"

"That's a crock," the five-year-old blurted, then quickly apologized.

"Where did you hear that phrase?" Asa smiled weakly as she asked, already knowing the answer.

Silence.

"Was it Daddy?" she smirked, holding back a laughing fit.

"Uh-huh," he whispered, still staring at the plastic stars glowing overhead.

"Figures," she whispered back.

"Why didn't you get the treatments?" The boy's tears suddenly ceased.

The sigh that escaped her felt as though it was filled with nails.

"If I had gotten the chemotherapy, there would be no Ava."

There was a long pause as they lay beside each other, hand in hand.

"Oh," he finally responded, resting his head on her shoulder and inhaling her rose scent.

"If your biological mother had listened to her moron of a boyfriend, Daddy and I wouldn't have you," she lovingly explained.

His tears lessened.

"Really?"

"Really." She kissed the top of his head and then continued. "If my parents hadn't moved from Detroit to Denver, I would never have met your dad, and we wouldn't be a family."

The little boy contemplated her words and then finally spoke.

"I love you, Mommy," he whispered against her shoulder; warm tears dampened her blouse, but she didn't care.

"I love you too, baby boy." Gently she squeezed his hand, trying to contain her tears, but couldn't. "I love you too."

Six months later…

Today, Dr. Khan's office was stuffy and stale. Not just because of the broken air conditioning system currently being worked on by an H-VAC technician but mainly because everyone in the room knew what was about to happen.

"The chemotherapy treatments aren't working," Dr. Khan's demeanor hardened, but his eyes blurred. Asa wasn't surprised. They had known each other almost her entire life.

"We tried," she comforted, being strong for all of them while holding back the onslaught of emotions threatening to consume her.

"We'll try a more aggressive treatment," Dr. Khan began. "I can send you to Arizona. A colleague of mine is the head of Oncology at—"

Shaking her head, she stood.

"I'm tired. It's been six months of… " she sighed. "I'm too tired to keep doing this."

Ian stood too, unsure of what else to do, of what else to say.

"Are you sure?" Ian probed, holding his own emotions in check as the severity of their situation sunk in. "You should sleep on it."

"I've already made up my mind," she spoke with a finality that made his knees shake.

Furious that she was giving up, he released her hand and made a beeline to the office door.

"Where are you going?" she called to his retreating back.

"I'll be in the car," he mumbled, refusing to make eye contact.

A few minutes later, she joined him in their vehicle, the windows up and the radio off. Needless to say, the ride back to their new home was long, tense, and miserable. Usually, she would stare out of the window at the passing scenery and marvel at the intensely colored shades of greens, blues, yellows, and muted earth tones. Normally, the beauty of Colorado would lift her spirit, but that was not the case this morning.

No. Today, nothing would comfort her. Nothing at all.

"Ian, aren't you going to talk to me?" Asa pleaded, needing to hear his voice.

Silence.

"So you're going to ignore me until I'm dead?"

The furious glare he gave made her shrink into the leather seat.

"Sorry," she whimpered, realizing it was a distasteful thing to say. "We have to tell Adam."

Still, no answer came from his direction.

"Ok, I'll speak with Adam," she sighed.

"No," he finally spoke. "I'll have to do it when you're gone anyway."

Touché.

"*Ouch,*" she mumbled, turning toward the window.

When they reached home, Ian bolted from the car and ran across the street to her parent's house to get the kids. Half an hour later, the three returned, accompanied by her mom and dad and the Grangers; everyone except Ava had red, swollen eyes.

Immediately, her mother hugged her and began to cry, making her cry as well. Her father just stared at her with a forlorn expression. All the while, her in-laws waited in turn to embrace her. Adam, on the other hand, ran upstairs, followed closely by his father.

Great!

Three months later…

"Smile, Asa," her dad encouraged.

"I look awful," she protested, covering her thin form with a blanket.

"You look just as crazy as you did when we were kids," her husband teased, earning him a hard slap to the arm.

"Mommy." Adam sat on her lap, waiting for another slice of birthday cake. "I'm going to be a chef and a photographer."

"I like the thought of that." Asa kissed his temple. "You can bake the cake, then take pictures of it."

"Yup," he grinned, taking the festive paper plate from his grandmother's hands.

"This is the best birthday party ever," she smiled from ear to ear. "But I'm tired, and I need to lie down."

Painstakingly she stood, kissed her parents and her in-laws, gave Adam and Ava kisses, too, and headed upstairs.

"Ian," Mr. Granger nudged him gently with his elbow. "Go upstairs with Asa. We'll clean up the mess. The kids can spend the night with us."

"Thanks," he murmured, waving goodbye to all of them before rushing upstairs.

"What took you so long?" Asa grilled, lounging on the bed in a long t-shirt, looking frail but just as beautiful to him.

Automatically, he rubbed his palm over his heart to subdue the ache.

"What are you doing?" His lopsided grin showed itself.

"Waiting to have my way with you," she purred.

"I thought you were tired?" He quickly stripped down to his underwear.

"I'm never too tired for that," she flirted, batting her long, dark lashes.

"Is that right," he growled playfully back.

"Get your delicious body over here before I change my mind." She patted the mattress beside her.

Grinning, he jumped onto the mattress and grabbed her around her small waist.

"You don't have to tell me twice."

"Easy," she reminded, giving a slight wince.

"Bossy," he teased.

Pulling his mouth to hers, she scoffed, "Always."

Epilogue

One year later…

"Huhwee, Adam," Ava shouted from the rooftop.

"It's pronounced *hurry,* not *huhwee,*" her big brother informed cheekily.

"No arguing, you two," Ian chastised as they waited for Adam to clear the ladder and join them on the long rectangular cushion. "Did you grab it?"

"Yes, sir," the boy revealed, handing the framed picture of the four of them: Ava, Adam, him, and Asa lying on the back lawn counting stars.

"Did you get the '*you-know-what*' from Grandma Keiko?"

"*Cookies!*" Ava clapped joyfully, making them laugh, dark brown eyes sparkling under the brightly lit sky, raven hair fluttering around her chubby cheeks. She was Asa in miniature, except healthy and strong.

Ian's heart clenched as he opened the *Tupperware* container and distributed two cookies each.

"Daddy, look!" Adam pointed at the sky. "It's the first meteor!"

"I want Mommy," Ava sulked, taking a big bite of one of her cookies.

"Me too." Ian pulled his daughter closer and surrounded her small frame with one arm.

During the course of her illness, Asa wrote lots of letters for him and their children for birthdays, holidays, and special occasions. They made home movies of all of their camping trips and vacations. Even daily activities that were once considered mundane took on new meaning as Asa interacted with them about photography and cooking and not being too rough on him as a single father.

She even recorded herself reading stories to them and talking to them about love and life.

"Me three," Adam's blue eyes glistened.

"Your mom and I looked at my first meteor shower from over there," he admitted, pointing to his in-law's roof. Asa's parents still couldn't bring themselves to perform the famous ritual yet.

He really couldn't blame them. It took all of his willpower to climb up on the roof and do it, but he knew that was what Asa expected him to do.

"Awesome," Adam chuckled.

"Did your mom tell you how we first met?"

Adam grinned and nodded yes before describing the story of her counting stars and of him harassing her.

"That's not how I remember it." Ian laughed. "Your crazy mother was up on the roof, and I was only trying to get her to safety."

"Mommy said you were scared of heights," Adam giggled.

"I still am," he admitted eating a cookie to take his mind off of where he was.

"Mommy sits by me."

Ava took the picture of the four of them and rested it beside her.

"Song… song," she reminded.

"I didn't forget, sweetheart," Ian grinned, pulling out his cell phone and finding the right tune to set the mood.

Slow introduction music by *One Republic* began to fade in, then quickly transformed into a lively rock ballad that his wife loved to sing along to.

So, in honor of her, he did:

"… Old, but I'm not that old Young, but I'm not that bold, I don't think the world is sold, I'm just doing what we're told,

"I feel something so right, Doing the wrong thing… I could lie, couldn't I, could lie,

"Everything that kills me makes me feel alive…."

The End.

About the Author

L. D. K. Johnson is an American author hailing from the East Coast of the U.S., where she enjoys spending time with family and friends when she is not sitting in front of her laptop writing the next book that comes to mind.

Her favorite things in life are chocolate, creamer (not necessarily coffee), and anything D.I.Y. related.

Available by L.D.K. Johnson

Claiming Kai

Episode #1 of The Kapahu Series

Available Everywhere!